TURN

TO HER

THE BROTHERS SERIES
BOOK TWO

Lynn Kellan

TURN TO HER

Book Two of The Brothers Series

This book is written in honor of the psychologists and health professionals who help so many people feel better. In particular, special thanks go to Dr. Matthew Kirkhart for his feedback, friendship, and cheerful willingness to answer tons of questions about how someone becomes a psychologist. Thank you, Matt!!

CHAPTER ONE

Fat, white snowflakes fell as though Old Man Winter had chopped up the moon and tossed the pieces to earth. A pair of headlights beamed through the snow, accompanied by an awful cough that belonged to an old sedan. The black car was hardly worth a second look, but Tia Garcia couldn't tear her gaze from the silhouette behind the steering wheel. That man lived next door to her and resembled a burly woodsman, the type who knew how to build campfires and track game in the brisk mountain air.

Days had passed since she'd spotted Mountain Man. Tia leaned closer to the cold window to get a better look. The tip of her nose tingled. So did her throat. A silky ribbon of goose bumps rolled toward her breasts.

Red taillights glowed as his sedan pulled into the empty parking space beside her car. Wouldn't take long before he walked into the apartment building. He'd say hello if he saw her. He always did.

Her heart did an excited little backflip. She pressed a hand against her chest and felt something fuzzy.

Lint.

The nasty gray stuff covered her black sweater. Her jeans looked worse, with a big wet glop of fabric softener on her upper thigh, near her crotch. To top things off, the laundry room's humidity had turned her long hair into rowdy ribbons of frizz.

If she were blonde, she might've been able to tell herself this was a good, breezy beach look. But she was a brunette. On her, brown frizz looked like a lonely Friday night spent all alone, washing clothes instead of hanging out at the bar like most of the graduate students on campus.

She grabbed her laundry basket, trotted into the apartment building's lobby, and headed for the stairs. Behind her, the lobby door opened with a shrill whine. Footsteps thudded on the tile floor. More goose bumps rose on Tia's skin, but she hurried upstairs without looking over her shoulder to see who was there. By the time she reached the second floor, her arms ached from hauling a big basket full of folded sweaters.

"Why are clean clothes heavier than dirty ones?" she muttered.

"You must not be washing them right."

Tia laughed and looked down the hall.

Wayne Hoover grinned back at her.

Mr. Buff, Blond, and Blunt was a psychology intern like her, but he leaned against her apartment door as though this drab, gray hallway was as pleasant as his sunny office in the Counseling Center. "Took you long enough to get here. I was beginning to think you got picked up by some guy."

"Nope. I was just doing laundry, which didn't go well. I'm covered in lint and fabric softener. I look like a woolly sheep with a bladder problem." She shoved the laundry basket into Wayne's arms and stuck her hand into her front pocket. It was empty. She reached into another pocket, and the bulky biofeedback band on her wrist caught the hem of her sweater. She yanked free. "Drat. I can't find my key."

"Did you leave it in the laundry room?"

"I hope not." She tried a back pocket. Sharp metal teeth grazed her knuckle. "Never mind. I got it." She unlocked the doorknob with a quick twist of her wrist, yanked Wayne into her apartment, and shut the door hard enough to rattle the picture on the wall.

He set the laundry basket on the couch and eyed her. "Uhhh, what's going on with you?"

"Nothing. I'm flustered, that's all. I'll be fine once I grab a cup of tea." She tucked a frizzy rope of hair behind one ear. "So, how did your seminar go?"

"Great. A lot of athletes attended. They all wanted to know how to use mental imagery to improve their performance. I used some of the exercises you'd suggested, which helped a lot. The football coach was there, too. He loved the whole thing." Wayne's mouth stretched into a wide smile. "He asked me to be the sports psychologist for the team."

"That's great news. Well done!"

"I want to celebrate. If you'll go to the bar with me, I'll buy you a drink."

A crisp Chardonnay would taste great right now, but she didn't have the time to go out. "I need to work. My internship hit a snag."

"What snag? You're the best counselor we've got. The girls flock to you for advice."

"I'm glad they do. Counseling is going well, but my seminar series for women is bothering some people."

Wayne's smile faded. "Yeah, I heard about that. Some guys have a problem with any program that excludes men. A few of them spoke to the Dean of Students. I overheard the discussion when I walked by."

So the rumors were true. Men were complaining about her program.

This wasn't good. All she wanted to do was help young women rely on themselves. She had to learn self-sufficiency the hard way when her father left the day before her eighth birthday, which was the worst present ever. Or maybe the best. Thanks to him, she could take care of herself.

She pressed her thumb against the wide silver ring on her index finger, reassured by the familiar smooth surface. "My seminars are designed specifically for women. I need to keep these seminars small and private so participants feel comfortable to talk about their problems, yet I don't want any man to feel excluded. Somehow, I've got to think of a way to make this work."

A lot was at stake. She'd developed this 'SelfWell'

program when her internship began last summer. If her program failed, she'd have trouble getting a post-doctoral job.

Psychologists were supposed to help people, not alienate them.

"You'll figure this out," Wayne said with a convincing nod. "But don't work all weekend. You need a break. Want to go skiing? Killington Peak is only an hour away and there's a ton of snow on the trails. That's the great thing about March in Vermont. There's always snow. Hit the trails with me."

"No, thanks. I don't ski." She'd navigated too many slippery slopes in her life. Skidding down a steep mountain on a pair of oversized blades sounded too much like her rocky childhood. "I appreciate your offer, but a quiet weekend at home will do me a lot of good."

Two firm knocks landed on the door.

Wayne scratched his head. "Are you expecting someone?"

"Nope." Tia looked through the blurry peephole. All she could see was a large blob. Since most of her friends looked like blurry blobs from this perspective, she opened the door.

Mountain Man stood three feet away, staring at her with vibrant blue eyes the color of Berry Blue gelatin—the flavor she'd used the one time she'd made gelatin shots. Those treats were packed with enough alcohol to deaden your tongue with one lick. Tia's tongue was nowhere near this man, yet her entire mouth went numb.

He removed a knit cap and pulled a hand through

his hair, ruffling thick brown curls. "A few seconds ago, I opened my car door too wide and dinged your passenger side door. I want to pay for the damage."

"Damage?" Her stomach dropped. She'd owned her SUV for five years and hadn't put one scratch on the shiny, black paint.

"The dent is small, no bigger than a nickel. A decent auto body shop can do the repair in a half hour, maybe less." He crushed the knit hat in one big hand. "This is my fault. My responsibility. I'll fix it."

"No, I'll handle this." She handled everything herself, the only way things got done.

"You will not handle the bill. I will."

Was he angry? Tia wasn't sure. His bright gaze gave nothing away and the thick pelt of his short beard cloaked the expressive muscles near his mouth, which was set in a straight, stony line.

An icy tingle trickled down her throat. She couldn't read this man.

He pulled a phone out of the back pocket of his jeans. "Could I have your number? I'd like to send you a screen shot of my insurance card in case you'd like to file a claim."

"Good idea." She rattled off her number.

He typed for a moment, put away his phone, and squared his shoulders. "I've lived near you for months, but I've never had the chance to introduce myself. I'm Ivan Antonov."

"I'm Tia Garcia." The rhyme in her name sounded silly compared to Mountain Man's name. *Ivan Antonov.* All of those hard consonants mimicked his voice, rough and deep. That sexy voice could talk an angel into trading her halo for a thong.

"I'd like to fix your car, soon. There's not much time left before I finish my Masters degree. After the semester ends, I won't be around. Until then, you can find me in one of the computer engineering labs." His frosty berry-blue eyes locked on hers. "I'm sorry for denting your car. I'll pay for everything."

"Thanks." She backed away from the threshold, anxious to get away before he noticed the smear of lint on her left boob.

"I'll touch base with you soon, Tia." Her name came out of his mouth in a hoarse murmur, softer than anything else he'd said.

"Okay. Bye." Jeez, did she just squeak? She closed the door and turned toward Wayne, who hadn't moved from his spot near the couch.

He grimaced. "I can't believe this."

"I know, right? This isn't a great way to start the weekend, but accidents happen." She shrugged, willing to look at the bright side of the situation. "At least the dent in my car is a small one."

"Forget about the stupid dent. You've got a bigger problem." Wayne jabbed a finger toward the door. "I saw your neighbor in the Dean's office a few days ago. He's the heartless jerk who wants to shut down your seminars."

CHAPTER TWO

Ivan dropped his gym bag beside the volleyball court and used the sleeve of his T-shirt to wipe off his face. He'd run to the gym in eleven minutes, ten seconds. A personal best. His thighs ached, his heart pounded, and he was covered in sleet and sweat. Felt good.

His high dipped when Henry 'Stretch' Gillette walked toward him with a sly grin. Looked like Stretch was about to fire some verbal bullets. Fine, then. Bring on the noise.

Ivan opened both hands. "What are you looking at?"

"Sweet sassy molassy, is that an icicle in your beard? You look like a frozen grizzly bear." Henry shoved a towel toward Ivan. "Dry off before you drip on the court."

"Yes, Mother." Ivan rubbed the rough terrycloth over his arms and legs.

"I can't imagine why you didn't drive here." Henry looked up at the gym's ceiling, pretending to give this some thought. "Let me guess. Did your sad excuse for a car refuse to start?"

"That's right. Sturdy Stella's engine flooded."

"You should trade in that thing for something better, like a dirty bucket on wheels."

"Ha-ha-larious." Ivan tossed the towel back to Henry.

"Isn't your brother a mechanic? Can't he fix Stella?"

"I won't ask Gabe to work on anything unless I can pay him, and right now I've got to fix someone else's car." Ivan held up one hand. "Don't ask. Long story."

He'd offered to repair Tia's car six days ago and hadn't seen her since then. Was she avoiding him, or just busy? Hard to say. Albrecht University was big enough to boast three academic quads, and Tia Garcia didn't stroll through the engineering quad very often. He usually crossed paths with her in the gym or in the lobby of the apartment building. No such luck, lately.

In six weeks, he'd never see her again. If he nailed his interview with Phoros Technologies, he'd move to Boston and start making real money doing computer design. He couldn't wait to leave campus. Once he got out of here, the familiar sting of his biggest mistake might finally fade away.

Henry picked up a volleyball. "Ready to play?"

"I will be, as soon as I can feel my fingers." Ivan flexed his left hand, but the biofeedback gadget around his wrist was tight enough to cut off some blood flow. He pushed a finger under the yellow wristband to ease the pressure. "How long do I have to wear this demonic device?"

"Three more days." Henry swatted Ivan's hand. "Quit messing with it. I spent months designing that marvel of engineering."

"Your so-called marvel is a misery. Can I loosen the band, at least?"

"Nope. The wristband has to be snug to measure your pulse, skin temperature, and muscle tension levels."

"The damned thing is tight enough to measure my thoughts." And none of them were noble at the moment, but Ivan would do anything for a good friend like Henry. Even if that meant being a guinea pig for some hare-brained experiment.

"I hope you're ready to kick some ass." Henry spun the volleyball on a long, bony finger. "I know this intramural league is supposed to be fun and all that garbage, but I want to win the cash prize."

"So do I." Ivan had planned to use his portion of the money to buy a new carburetor for his car, but Sturdy Stella would have to wait until he fixed the dent in Tia's SUV. "Who are we playing?"

"Some team called The Freudian Slips. They're undefeated, so don't get too cocky."

"The Freudian Slips?" A sick feeling twisted in his stomach. "What are they, a bunch of shrinks?"

"Yeah, I guess. They're from the Department of Psychology."

"Damn." The last thing he wanted to do was face a bunch of two-faced therapists. They'd misinterpret every word that dropped out of his mouth. "This'll be a long game. After every point, these asinine shrinks will probably want to know how we *feel.*"

Henry laughed. "I'd better talk to their captain and see how he feels about starting the game."

"He's probably that tall guy with the David Beckham hair." Typical. All style and no substance. Disgusted, Ivan reached into his gym bag for a bottle of water.

That's when he spotted her. She had perfect thighs that contained a mouthwatering curve near her hips. He'd memorized that shape months ago, when an unusually warm shot of air had bled into campus. On that blessed day, Tia Garcia had walked into the gym in shorts, but not as short as the ones she wore now. These were made out of dark, stretchy material that hugged her hips so well, he wanted to fall on both knees to worship the stellar view.

She stopped right in front of him, which was something new.

He treated himself to a brief glance at her breasts, which were covered by a white T-shirt. The pretty curves beneath all of that fabric gave him a whole new appreciation for cotton.

Tia crossed her arms over her chest. "What were you saying about my team?"

Shit. Houston, we have a problem. "Just a bunch of trash talk."

"Your trash talk sounded like a bona fide insult, but don't stop. I play better when I'm angry."

"Stick with me and you'll play like an All-American." The joke didn't make her smile. There could be only one reason for that. She was one of them. A shrink. "Are you part of the psychology program?"

"Yep. I'm an intern. While I'm here, I'm offering a series of seminars for women." Her eyes narrowed into two slits of anger. "The type of seminars you oppose."

"What?"

"You heard me." She walked past him.

God, not this. Not her. He reached her in two angry strides. "Are you part of those no-men-allowed seminars offered by The Women's Grid?"

"No. My program is sponsored by the Counseling Center."

"Then you have nothing to worry about. I'm going after The Women's Grid. Those shrews spew man-hate all over campus, and I'm going to stop them." This battle was personal. The women in The Grid had spread terrible rumors about him. That wouldn't happen again, to anyone. He'd dismantle The Women's Grid and anything else like it. "I've got a problem with any program on campus that targets men."

"How do you know whether or not a program *targets* men?"

"I check to see if men are welcome to participate in the program. If the answer is no, there's a problem."

"That's ridiculous. If I want to give women the chance to talk about a sensitive topic in a private setting, I'm not targeting men." Tia pulled her hair into a ponytail with a brusque yank.

Ivan leaned back to avoid being hit by the thick rope of her hair. "Listen, I might've oversimplified—"

"Forget it. I'm too angry to have a reasonable conversation right now."

Yeah, she was pissed. A bright flush flamed in her pretty face and those dark eyes of hers wouldn't met his. "Are you angry because I dinged your car or because I want every program on campus to be inclusive?"

"To be honest, your pithy little quip about shrinks really got to me."

"Pithy? I can't remember the last time I heard someone use that word." Or the last time someone answered his questions with such quick honesty. "Sorry about the shrink comment."

"You don't sound sorry." She turned toward him so fast, her sneakers squealed. "I'm a psychologist, not a shrink. I've completed four years of graduate work toward my Ph.D. I'm almost done with my internship, and then I'll pursue a post-doc position, which means I'll complete more than six years of training before I practice. How many years does your degree require? Two?"

That small number dropped out of her perfect mouth like a sour raisin. Okay, he might not have spent as much time in graduate school as she had, but he'd gotten into Mensa when he was in high school and he'd aced the SAT, ACT, and GRE exams. When he played hockey for Boston College, he carried a perfect 4.0 grade point average and was an Academic All-American. Those feats might prove his worth to her, but he was damned tired of being admired for his intellect and nothing else. "Let's not compare programs. Everyone knows an advanced degree in computer engineering requires a different skill set than anything in the social sciences."

Her jaw firmed. "I see."

"What, exactly, do you see?" He shouldn't have asked, because she fired a long look at him. Being on the receiving end of all that gorgeous irritation made his cock throb inside his jock strap.

"Take your positions," Henry hollered. "The final match of the graduate school's intramural league is about to begin."

Ivan took his customary position at the net and watched Tia move into the spot directly across from him. Looked like she wanted to slap him.

Damn. He wanted to impress her, not anger her. First, he'd dented her car. And now this. He was so hot for this woman, his brain short-circuited every time he got near her or her car.

A serve zinged over the net. Ivan's teammate passed the ball to Henry, who hit the ball deep into the Freudian Slips' court. Someone in the back row bumped a pass toward Tia. She jumped and executed a perfect spike.

The ball blasted into Ivan's chest and ricocheted out of bounds.

"One point down." Tia brushed off her hands and peered through the net at Ivan. "How do you *feel*?"

"Surprised. Impressed." He leaned until the tip of his nose was a couple of inches from hers. "You bruised my chest."

She flicked the curly ends of her ponytail over one shoulder. "Get ready for more, Mountain Man."

Huh, he'd never been called that before. The nickname fit. Curious to see what else she'd do, he opened his arms wide. "Come at me, Doc."

Another serve flew over the net. Henry dove in time to bump the ball into the air, close to the net. Tia leapt and drilled another shot at Ivan.

He lunged to avoid getting nailed in the face. The ball

slammed into his shoulder and flew out of reach. A sting charged across his collarbone like an electric bolt, jagged and hot. By the time Ivan regained his footing, he knew he was in trouble. This woman was strong enough to show him exactly who she was, which provoked a feeling he hadn't experienced in months.

Fascination, bone-deep and irresistible.

CHAPTER THREE

Twenty-four hours after losing that epic volleyball game, Ivan trudged to the fifth floor of his apartment building. God, he was hungry. The peanut butter sandwich he'd shoved into his mouth for dinner felt as filling as a stale marshmallow, but he couldn't afford to get take-out now that he'd lost the chance to win the intramural league's cash prize. No big deal. If he cut back on groceries, he'd have enough money to fix the dent in Tia's car.

He'd eat nothing but peanut butter for the next two weeks if that bought him another chance to see her. Cheered by the thought, he stopped in front of Henry's apartment and knocked twice.

An attractive redhead opened the door. "Oh, good. You must be Ivan. We're almost ready to start." She pointed to the yellow band around his wrist. "Have you had any trouble with your biofeedback device during the past few days?"

"The band is a little tight. Other than that, no problem."

"Terrific. I'll tell Annette you're here. Come inside."

This was the first time he'd had to get past a perky little gatekeeper to set foot in Henry's place. The living room was filled with people who looked to be in their twenties, graduate students like him who'd volunteered to do this goofy experiment.

Henry was seated at a small table near the corner of the room. Ivan plopped into a nearby chair and glanced at his friend's open laptop. Numbers and graphs flickered on the monitor. "Looks like you're measuring the pulse of every living soul on the planet."

"I've collected enough data over the past week to plot the pulse readings, activity levels, and sleep patterns of everyone in this experiment." Henry pointed a brief, worried squint at him. "You average four hours of sleep a night. Zombies get more rest than you do."

"They don't have as much work as I do." If a zombie could write the article he wanted to submit to the Journal of Electrical Engineering, he'd gladly hand his thumb drive to the undead. "How long is this going to take?"

Henry muttered a curse. "Didn't you read the directions?"

"I didn't have time."

"All right, just go with the flow." Henry stopped scrolling through data and glanced to his left. "Did you see her?"

The slight crack in the word *her* caught Ivan's attention. "Who?"

"Tia Garcia. She's part of the experiment, too. Didn't you see that she was wearing a wristband like yours?"

"I was too busy dodging volleyballs to gawk at her wrist." But he'd gawked at other parts of her when they'd faced-off last night. Hungry for another eyeful, Ivan looked around the room but didn't spot a tall, stunning brunette. "Where is she?"

"In the kitchen."

"Great. She must be picking out a heavy pan to swing at me."

"Why? Wait, I can guess. You pissed her off." Henry leaned back and sighed. "What did you do?"

"I called her a shrink." And he wasn't proud of that. He'd offended the woman who starred in all of his fantasies. Those fantasies were the best part of his empty nights. "Apparently, psychologists don't like being called shrinks."

"Go figure." Five bony fingers drummed on the table. "Maybe she'll forgive and forget."

"Not likely. She knows I went to the Dean to complain about the women-only seminars that keep popping up on campus. Turns out, Tia runs a seminar series for women."

"Oh, that's rich. You went after those hateful hags in The Women's Grid and pulled Tia into that mess."

"Something like that." Which explained why she'd walked away after the intramural game without a simple goodbye. He recalled the wary anger in her gaze and felt his insides clench. "Did you know she played volleyball in college? I did a simple Google search last night and found her all over the web. She was an Academic All-American at Middlebury College, where she got that killer spike. That spike bruised my chest and my ego, but the rest of me can't wait to see her again."

"Then this is your lucky day." Henry's voice dropped to a low murmur, the tone he used whenever he had something important to say. "In a few minutes, you'll be paired with her."

"Great." Ivan's grin died a quick death when he noticed a twitch of worry on his friend's face. "Does Tia know she'll be with me?"

"Uh, no, but everything will work out." Henry smiled too wide and clapped Ivan on the shoulder. "Everything will work out."

"You're repeating yourself, which means you're convinced everything will fall apart."

"Just shut up and listen." Henry's gaze swung to a petite blonde who walked toward the front of the room.

She gave a friendly wave. "Hello, everyone. I'm Annette Farrington. As you probably know, I'm the psychology intern who designed this experiment. Thank you for agreeing to participate."

The low murmur of conversation in the room dropped to a curious hush.

"With your help, we hope to learn how physical proximity to another person affects our well-being. If we can quantify how being close to someone affects us, we might figure out new ways to treat conditions like depression. In order to gather data, we've collaborated with the Department of Computer Engineering to design the measuring devices on your wrists." Annette pointed a warm smile toward Henry. "Working together has been enormously successful."

Henry grinned back at her and turned tomato red.

"For the past few days, we've measured your temperature, perspiration, blood pressure, and pulse so we can get to know you. We'll compare those results to the measurements produced by tonight's exercise. In this phase, we're testing to see how physical proximity affects people who don't know each other well. Once we pair you up, you'll go through a series of steps based on research done by Desmond Morris, who wrote a number of books on sociobiology." Annette gestured to the redhead who'd answered the door. "Kristin, would you help me guide everyone to their seats?"

As everyone changed positions, Ivan caught sight of Tia. She had a brief conversation with Annette, walked to the couch, and sat down.

Henry nudged Ivan's arm. "Put your ass in that empty chair across from Tia. Try to be nice."

"Being nice won't be a problem." Anticipation kicked a potent dose of adrenaline into his bloodstream. His pulse banged against the yellow band cinched around his wrist. Heat raced up the back of his neck and bled into the shells of his ears. He shouldered past Henry and strode toward the couch, his mind racing with possibilities and probabilities.

The moment he stepped in front of Tia, everything buffered into slow motion.

She looked up at him and sucked in a short, surprised gasp. Her hands curled into two tight fists in her lap, her knuckles white against tawny skin.

He sat down, positioning his legs on either side of her knees. Even though his body penned her in, he was the one who felt trapped, caught up in a snarl of want and agitation.

"Do not say anything at this time." Annette glanced at a stopwatch. "Just take a moment to observe your partner. This is a quiet observational moment, much like when you first notice someone. I know this may feel awkward or silly, but rest assured that whatever you feel is okay. This step will last for thirty seconds. You may begin."

Ivan already knew what Tia looked like, but he welcomed the chance for a close inspection. She was wearing boots, as usual, but these were made of black leather that went all the way up to her knees. So damned hot. Dark denim hugged her lean thighs and accentuated the curve of her hips. On top of all that, she wore a simple white blouse that made her look bank-teller classy and beach-lifeguard sexy at the same time. Loose chestnut waves framed her breathtaking face and her lips were a soft pink color, full and lush.

Tia's gaze skipped to the small hole in the knee of his jeans, drifted up the front of his faded denim shirt, and landed on his beard. A narrow crease formed along her forehead.

She didn't look angry. More like baffled.

Had she spotted something odd? Ivan pulled a hand across his jaw, half-expecting to find something wrong. Nope. Nothing but short whiskers. He might look like a Mountain Man, but at least he was a well-groomed one.

Annette voice rose. "For our next step, look into each other's eyes. This phase might make you feel uncomfortable or ill-at-ease, but that's all right. We'll only hold this pose for a short ten seconds. Ready, go."

Ivan gazed into Tia's eyes and his mind switched to Slovak, the language his parents spoke at home. Being this close to Tia Garcia drained all of the English out of his head. He snapped out of his fog with two simple thoughts.

Only a few weeks until graduation.

Stay focused.

"Very good. Let's proceed to the next step." Annette checked the paperwork on her clipboard. "Closeness is fostered by good communication, so we're going to give you some time to start a conversation. Go ahead and say whatever comes to mind."

Tia tilted her head. "You don't strike me as the type who'd volunteer for this type of exercise. Why are you here?"

"I agreed to do this for a friend."

"Hm." Her gaze drifted to the front of the room. "For Annette? Or Kristin?"

"Neither. Henry asked for my help, and I resent the implication that I'm here in some idiotic attempt to impress a woman." Damn, that sounded angry. Not nice at all.

Her eyebrow twitched. So did the corner of her mouth. "Ah. I see."

"You said that before, when we played volleyball." He disliked the phrase. A lot. It reminded him of the sanctimonious therapist he'd met eight months ago. Old anger flared, forcing out words before he had the chance to filter them. "I'm not fluent in psychobabble. What does *I see* mean?"

"It means I understand what you said." She tossed her hair behind one shoulder with a quick flick of her wrist. "By the way, psychobabble isn't a thing."

"Could've fooled me." His knee bumped against hers. The contact jolted a sensual sizzle up his leg. He dug an elbow into his thigh to stop the sensation from reaching his crotch, which was pointless. His dick knew what his knee had done and wanted more. "Maybe you can answer a question for me. How can a psychologist draw conclusions if she only hears her client's side of the story? That's just half of the facts. Shouldn't members of your profession gather more data before reaching a judgment?"

Her gaze darkened, as ominous as the barrel of a shotgun. "I'd be happy to discuss the principles of effective psychotherapy some other time."

"Fine. What time works for you, Doc?" He leaned forward, close enough to feel the startled pant of her breath against the tip of his nose. "Should I initiate this discussion when you're hurrying away from me when we cross paths at the gym, or when you sprint upstairs the moment I step into our building's lobby?"

Her jaw dropped. A pink flush appeared on the bridge of her nose. The blush drifted outward, stretching along the ridge of her cheekbones.

He'd surprised her.

Embarrassed her, too.

Way to go, Einstein.

Annette's voice rose above the chatter. "At this point in the experiment, you'll begin to touch each other. While we proceed, you may incorporate previous steps to enhance your comfort levels. For instance, if you'd like to continue talking, that's fine. When you're ready, hold your partner's hand."

Fat chance that would happen. Tia probably wanted to strangle him, not hold him.

Ivan looked down at the meaty hands he'd inherited from his ancestors. Those men were reticent, durable farmers who'd carved out an existence cultivating the valleys in Slovakia. Even though he resembled those sturdy men, he was nothing like them. He was an aberration. A sharp tack in a box of stout nails. A prodigy who'd mastered simple calculus when he was five years old. A kid who skipped two grades in elementary school and double-majored in college. The only smartass in the family who couldn't keep his big mouth shut.

Until now. He had no idea what to say.

Might as well start with the truth. "I'm acting like a first-class jerk."

She lifted one shoulder in a small shrug. Her quiet gaze stayed on his.

Not the reaction he expected, but he was beginning to suspect Tia was the type of person who listened, even when she was mad.

He swallowed, but had no spit. "I'm lashing out at you because I'm angry. Not at you, but at someone else. She was a therapist. I tried to speak with her a few months ago, but she wouldn't listen to what I had to say. She didn't want my side of the story. Whatever I had to say didn't matter."

That woman claimed he was 'heartless.' No one had ever called him that.

It hurt. Badly.

"I assume every therapist is like the one I met, which isn't fair." He pressed his hands together and cracked a knuckle, but the familiar habit didn't make him feel any better. "Last night, I called you a shrink. I insulted you and your program. Today, my behavior didn't improve. I ripped into you for no good reason. I never should've attacked you like that. I wish I'd treated you with more respect. I'm sorry, Tia."

Her eyes widened, earnest and warm. "I'm sorry, too. For spiking the ball at you last night." She winced. "One shot almost hit you in the head."

"Don't sweat it. I play a lot of hockey, so I'm used to dodging shots." He placed a hand on top of hers. "You did nothing wrong, Tia. I'm the one at fault."

She laced her fingers through his and delivered a soft squeeze. "Thank you for telling me what's going on. You have good reason to feel angry. I wish that therapist had been able to listen to you. We all need someone who is willing to hear our side of the story."

Astounded by her kindness, he brushed his thumb across her skin. She felt like silk against the rough burlap of his callouses. Cradling her hand in both of his, he studied the wide silver ring on her index finger. The band contained a jagged design that reminded him of a mountain ridge. The peaks looked familiar. He touched the ring. "Did you buy this in Wyoming?"

"Yes. How did you know?"

"The etching looks like the Teton Mountains. I saw them when I was seven."

A puzzled pucker formed between her eyebrows. "You remember what the mountains looked like from so long ago?"

"Tough to forget a sight like that." For him, at least. He remembered everything, which was why he aced every test and flunked every relationship.

"Time to move on," Annette said. "We'll need you to stand for this next step."

Ivan groaned. "How many steps are in this experiment?"

Tia pulled her hand out of his. "Didn't you read the material?"

"No. I've been elbow-deep in work. I didn't have time to prepare for this."

She tilted her head again. "Yet you had time to play volleyball last night."

"That game was important."

An amused smile bloomed on her mouth. "I see."

"Stop saying that," he grouched, aiming a mild glare at her.

"Sorry. I couldn't resist." She got up and tugged his sleeve. "Get on your feet, Mountain Man. We've got eight more steps to work through."

"Eight? This is going to take forever." He stood. A

faint throb pinged the back of his eyes, the beginning of a headache.

Tia nudged him. "Hey, this isn't going to be so bad. We can do this."

Damn, her optimism was dangerous. If she gave him that we-can-do-this look and asked for something, there was a very good chance he'd say yes.

"For our fifth step, we're going to ask the men to put one arm around your partner's shoulders. Hold this position until I ask you to stop. Ready?" Annette scanned the couples until her gaze landed on Ivan. "Go ahead."

Fine, then. Ivan wound one arm around Tia's shoulders. She was definitely taller than most women. Felt strange to tilt his head down a scant degree to meet her gaze. Up this close, he could see gold flecks in her brown eyes.

He curled his fingers around her upper arm, able to feel the heat from her body through the thin fabric of her blouse. Her hair brushed a silky caress along his forearm. Everything about this woman felt good. Too bad she was a therapist. Would she misjudge him like the other one did?

"You're frowning," she murmured.

"I frown a lot." So he'd been told.

"Why?"

"Do you always ask so many questions?"

An impish light appeared in her eyes. "Does that bother you?"

"Only when you answer one of my questions with a question." He smirked, but stopped when she blurred a little bit. He pinched the bridge of his nose to distract himself from the ache behind his eyes. If he took out his contacts, the pain might recede.

"Time's up. Release your partner," Annette said. "Ladies, it's your turn. Place your arm around your partner's shoulders. If you can't reach that high, an arm around his upper back is acceptable."

Tia looped an arm around his shoulders.

Ivan gazed at the honeyed skin of her neck. Below the hollow of her throat, there were three little freckles. If he connected them with a line, they'd make an isosceles triangle that pointed to her left breast. He wanted to lick those freckles. Better yet, kiss them. Maybe find out if she'd squirm. Or moan.

"You park next to my car a lot," she said.

"Uh, yeah." He studied the scuff on the toe of his boots and tried to act bored, which was impossible to do with Tia Garcia around.

"Someone has been clearing the snow off my windshield. I finally figured out who." She dipped her head to catch his gaze. "You're the one. I saw you clean off my car this morning."

Busted. "No big deal. The snow was easy to remove."

"Looked icy and heavy to me."

Didn't matter. Doing something nice for her felt good, but he hadn't wanted her to find out. He didn't want her to feel obligated to return the kindness. Obligation sucked. "I have to wait for my car to warm up every morning, so I scrape your windshield and mine to kill the time. Like I said, it's no big deal."

"Well, I just wanted to say thanks. Your thoughtfulness

has saved me a lot of time and trouble." She smiled.

The open gratitude in her gaze made every second he'd spent in the bitter cold worthwhile. He smiled back at her. "You're welcome."

"Now we'll move on to the sixth step," Annette announced. "Place an arm around your partner's waist and give him or her a small squeeze around the waist."

Ivan moved at the same time Tia did. Their hands bumped.

"This is boring. Let's move on to the next step," a man said.

Nervous chuckles filled the room.

"Well, since you asked, the seventh step is a simple kiss. In real life, you have a good chance of kissing someone if you've taken the time to go through the six previous steps, but we're accelerating things for the sake of our experiment. Go ahead and kiss your partner. One brief touch of the lips will do."

Ivan couldn't believe it. "They want us to kiss?"

"Yes." A vivid flush washed across Tia's face.

Everything inside him flared like hot wire, coppery red and smoking. He grabbed her around the waist and pressed his mouth against her soft, pink lips. She tasted like sweet tea and cinnamon cookies. A lifetime had passed since he'd put either of those things into his system.

She jerked back, her brown eyes almost as big as ping pong balls.

"Step eight is next," Annette said. "Touch your partner's face. A gentle caress on the chin or cheek is fine."

"On it." He stroked a fingertip along Tia's silky cheek. If this experiment gave him permission to touch this woman, he was all in. Anything for science, right?

She wasn't touching him, though. She wasn't talking, either. She wasn't doing anything except staring down at her hands as though she wasn't sure where to put them.

He lowered his hand. "We'd better keep up. Your turn."

"Right. Sorry. Here goes." She pressed two gentle fingertips against his jaw. "Hm. Not only do your whiskers look thick, they feel thick."

"Which is why I grew them. They hide a scar." He pointed to his chin. "I got biffed by a hockey puck a couple of years ago."

"So you grew a beard to cover the scar?" Her fingers explored that spot.

A shiver of pure pleasure coasted along his jaw. "Yeah. I got tired of telling people about how I got hurt. Plus, I don't like to shave every day."

"I know. Shaving is the worst." She lowered her hand and twisted the ring on her finger. "I mean, if I was a guy, I wouldn't like to shave my face every day."

"I get what you're trying to say." But that didn't stop him from wondering what parts she shaved, and how often.

"We've reached the final four steps," Annette announced. "We're going to breeze through them to keep things simple. For the ninth step, we're going to ask the men to place one hand on his partner's abdomen, on top of her clothing."

Ivan gazed down to make sure he didn't touch

something he shouldn't, and caught got a distracting glimpse of Tia's cleavage. Definitely B cups, maybe slightly bigger. The perfect size for him. The throb in his crotch became a full-fledged ache, making it difficult to concentrate on finding a safe spot on her blouse that was a respectful distance from her breasts yet not too close to the fly of her jeans. He placed his hand where he thought her belly button might be and felt a distinct tremble beneath his palm.

Hell, she looked pale. And scared.

"You're shaking." *Shit.* The last thing he wanted to do was frighten this woman. He pulled his hand away. "Do you want to stop?"

"No. This is important. I can keep going." She gripped his forearm like she needed something to hold on to. "I'm just nervous. I haven't gotten close to someone in a while."

He knew that. For the past six months, he hadn't seen Tia with anyone except for that blond guy who she treated like a friend, not a date.

"The tenth step involves kissing your partner's bare chest." Annette checked her paperwork. "For this step, we'll ask the ladies to kiss the base of your partner's neck to achieve this level of physical closeness."

Ivan wasn't sure Tia could move, much less kiss him. He put one arm around her, gave her back a reassuring pat, and leaned down until his forehead got close to hers. "You don't have to do anything. We can stay like this."

"I can't stop. I promised to do this experiment for my friends, so…" She spread open his collar and brushed her lips against his throat.

Heat skated down Ivan's chest on sharp blades. Lust zinged into his groin. His vision blurred, smudging everything but Tia. The deadly numbness inside him vanished. He was alive again, amped up like a lithium battery. Hot need made him want to seize her mouth, shove his hands under her shirt, press his thick dick against her slim curves.

Rotten idea. She was nervous, uncertain, and uncomfortable. Her distress would skyrocket if he acted like a horny caveman. He released her and eased away.

"We've reached the final two steps," Annette announced, all chirpy enthusiasm. "If you'd gone through all of these steps in real life, this might be the time you'd touch your partner intimately. Don't worry. We're not going to ask you to do anything overtly sexual."

A guy paired with an attractive blonde raised one fist into the air with an exuberant whoop. "Time to go south of the equator!"

People laughed.

Ivan didn't. If Tia explored below his belt, she'd find irrefutable evidence that this dimwitted experiment had gotten alarmingly real for him.

"Our next step is fairly simple," Annette explained. "Place one hand into your partner's back pocket."

Even though he'd just been handed permission to palm Tia Garcia's curvy little ass, he grabbed her elbow and felt another tremor. "This is crazy, Tia. I'm not going to grab your backside without your permission. You're not some plaything. I'm not going to screw with you."

A small noise came out of her, something close to

a surprised hiccup. She slid her hand into his, her grip tight.

Warmth spread within his chest. He tried to identify the emotion that accompanied the feeling. This was stronger than surprise. More like awe. She'd reached for his hand because she wanted to hold onto him. That meant a lot.

"We've reached our final step," Annette said. "You've touched your partners on most of their intimate areas: hands, shoulders, waist, lips, face, abdomen, chest, and butt. That leaves the genitals. Needless to say, we won't ask you to go that far. Just give your partner a tight hug that will press your lower halves together."

Tia curled one hand around the back of his neck and looped her other arm around his shoulders to pull close. Her velvety cheek pressed against his. The dizzying scents of cinnamon cookies and tea drifted into his nose. Soft breasts flattened against his chest. Slender hips cradled his raging hard-on.

Felt so effing good.

He clenched his jaw to muffle a moan. A hard twinge pinged in the roots of his molars, a good reminder that he should leave Tia alone. She was a psychologist, for crying out loud. If she was as inept as the other one he'd met, she'd never listen to him. If she was a good one, she'd realize he was toast, charred from one bad night.

He yanked out of the embrace.

"The next phase of our experiment will last for four hours. All you have to do is stay close to your partner, which means you'll need to wear this." Annette removed the lid from a shoebox and emptied the contents. Five handcuffs clattered onto the coffee table.

CHAPTER FOUR

Tia slapped one handcuff around Ivan's wrist even though she knew something was wrong. Ivan's big body seemed to contain the precarious balance of a boulder on the edge of a cliff. Any second now, he'd gather speed and tumble out of here.

This man baffled her. He'd been so sweet to her right before he'd yanked out of her hug. Now he wouldn't look at her. Those lips of his formed a stern, straight line. His thick beard shielded most of the lower half of his face. His stoic expression gave nothing away.

Every time she saw that look on a man, her mind went blank. She didn't know how to interpret that hard gaze and jutting jaw. Was he angry? Frustrated? Embarrassed? She couldn't tell.

She had to overcome this mental block. A good psychologist could serve a large range of clients. Young and old. Shy and bold. Male and female.

Females were easy to understand. Males, not so much. They intrigued her, but she'd never had the chance to spend much time with them. The only man she'd known for a decent amount of time was her father, and she hadn't been able to spot his unhappiness until it was too late.

A tingle wiggled up her throat. Her sinuses began to fill. If she didn't pull herself together, a ribbon of snot would roll out of her nose, which was her body's way of dealing with stress. Kind of like crying, but without tears. It was awful. Humiliating, really.

She gave Ivan as much room as she could, which wasn't much now that a six-inch chain linked them together. "I know you didn't have time to read about the experiment, but the worst is over. All we have to do is stay close to each other until midnight."

"Fine, but why do we have to wear handcuffs?"

"They'll force us into each other's personal space, which is the point of the experiment—to test how physical proximity affects people."

Ivan dragged his free hand down his face. "I thought this wouldn't last more than an hour. I've got to work."

"In your lab?"

"No, I need to write something."

Whatever he had to write must be important. Around here, most graduate students didn't work on Friday nights. "Do you need to finish a paper?"

"Kind of. I have to write an article for the Journal of Engineering. The editor wants me to talk about the hybrid fuel cell I designed." He pinched the bridge of his nose and shrugged. "I need to submit the draft by midnight."

"We can find a quiet spot where you can write." She injected a hearty amount of optimism into her voice. "I'll work, too."

Ivan scowled at the handcuff as though he wanted to break free. Judging by the size of his powerful forearm, he could bust the thin silver chain with one firm yank.

That couldn't happen. Tia needed him to stay. She'd promised to be a part of the experiment to help Annette and Kristen. Both women were psychology interns, like her. She relied on them for support and wanted to support them too, but she wasn't too happy about being paired with Ivan. He'd thrown a major stumbling block into her internship when he'd gone to the Dean to criticize the women-only seminars on campus.

Then again, this might be a good chance to explain why her self-sufficiency seminars needed to focus on women. If she had to handcuff herself to Mountain Man to get him to listen, she'd do so. Didn't matter that when she'd hugged him, her hips bumped into a hard bulge as big as Vermont. She could forget about that.

As if.

"You can unlock the shackles in case you need to separate for bio breaks." Annette handed a key to Ivan, another key to Tia, and moved on to the couple who stood at the opposite end of the couch. "Remain in the building so we can reach you if there's a problem. Feel free to hang out with friends to pass the time."

A man waved his hand. "I live down the hall. I've got a huge flat screen television and plenty of movies to watch. Everyone is welcome."

That option didn't seem to appeal to Ivan, who hadn't pocketed his key.

"Want to hang out in my apartment?" she offered. "My place is quiet. We can work there."

"Fine." He lurched into motion and swung away from the couch.

Tia lengthened her stride to keep up with him. Near the door, she paused to wave goodbye to Annette and Kristin. The handcuff dug into her wrist, hard. She stumbled and clutched a handful of Ivan's shirt to keep upright.

He threw a frown over his shoulder.

"Sorry. Lost my balance." She let go of his shirt, leaving a wrinkle where she'd grabbed him.

He lifted a hand to his jaw. The handcuff yanked her hand along for the ride.

"Damn." He lowered his arm.

The back of Tia's hand bumped into his hip. She jerked away from the soft denim. The bumpy row of Ivan's knuckles collided into her thigh.

"Let's go." He seized her hand, pulled her out of the apartment, and accelerated toward the stairwell. The brisk pace continued down three flights of steps with his blunt fingers tight around her palm and the handcuff pressed against her forearm. By the time they arrived at the second floor, a hard crease formed above the thick slash of his eyebrows and his spine was as hard and straight as the hallway walls.

In front of his apartment, Ivan jammed the key into his handcuff. The manacle opened with a soft snick. The empty cuff banged into Tia's forearm.

She gaped at him. "What are you doing?"

"Go to your place. I'll be there in a minute." He walked into his apartment and shut the door.

"But—" Tia stared at the numbers tacked to his door. Two-zero-seven. Some of the black paint had flecked off of the seven, exposing the silver metal underneath.

Staring at his door in mute disbelief wouldn't change anything, so she walked a short distance down the hallway and entered her apartment. As usual, she placed her boots by the door and put the empty manacles, her keys, and her phone on the shelf where she kept her things, but the comforting routine of returning home felt hollow. If Ivan had just quit on her, she had no idea why.

That's the reason she wanted to become a psychologist in the first place, so she could understand why people acted the way they did. She hadn't made much progress. Her search for answers always seemed to produce more questions.

What was going on with Ivan? He'd seemed okay with the experiment. As the steps progressed, he'd become more engaged. He'd even noticed her nervousness and treated her with gentle care.

You're not some plaything. I'm not going to screw with you.

Ivan hadn't jumped at the chance to cop a quick feel. Well, except for the kiss. That was a surprise. A good one. That kiss contained a raw, hungry heat that was a heady contradiction to the tender way he handled her. If he didn't mind getting close, why had he pulled away?

She needed tea. A hot cup of Earl Grey might thaw the cold knot in her stomach.

Two brusque knocks landed on her door. "Tia, it's me. Ivan."

That low, gravelly voice couldn't belong to anyone else. She backtracked out of the kitchen and opened the door.

Ivan peered at her through a pair of tortoiseshell glasses. "My contact lenses were killing me, so I took them out."

"Oh. Okay." Holy mother of all things manly, those glasses made him look like a hot professor who knew how to make any topic interesting.

He shrugged and opened one hand. "What?"

"I wasn't sure you'd return," Tia admitted, mentally rolling her tongue back into her mouth. This studious version of Mountain Man made all of her soft parts tingle. Not only because he looked great, but because he'd kept his word. He showed up, just like he said he would.

"So…" He hooked a thumb under the worn strap of the knapsack draped over his big shoulder. "Are we doing this experiment or not?"

"Yes. Come in."

He stepped inside, tugged off his boots, and placed them on the shoe tray near the door. That done, he shot a curious look toward the kitchen. "I smell cinnamon."

"You probably smell biscochitos," she guessed.

"Bisco-what?"

"Biscochitos. Mexican sugar cookies, from my mother's recipe. I baked some after dinner. Want one?"

"Thanks, but no. Better not." He looked around and

nodded toward the living room. "May I sit on the couch?"

"Of course. Would you like something to drink?"

"Water would be good, please."

This strained politeness felt unnatural, but Tia couldn't tell if Ivan was nervous or if she was the only one freaking out. She retreated to the kitchen to grab some waters and paused by the counter. Soon, she'd have to handcuff him again. The big guy wouldn't like that.

Cookies might help.

With the plate of biscochitos in hand, she grabbed the handcuffs on her way back into the living room. She placed the food on the coffee table and dangled the manacles from her finger. "We have to put these back on."

He stopped digging into his backpack and looked up. "Damn, not those again."

"We agreed to wear them when we consented to participate in the experiment."

"You agreed. I had no idea what I was getting myself into."

"Good point, but that doesn't change the parameters of the experiment. Annette and Kristin need us to wear these for four hours."

"Four hours? Man, I should've read that documentation. Fine, whatever." He rolled up his sleeves and extended one arm.

She cuffed him, which wasn't easy. The manacle barely fit around his thick wrist. After snapping the other cuff on herself, she sat on the couch beside him. "Thank you for doing this. Now the experiment will have data from five couples."

"If this experiment is supposed to study people who don't know one another, we don't belong together." He looked at her, his eyes bright blue behind his glasses. "You're no stranger to me."

"I'm not sure what you mean. We may live next door to one another, but we don't know each other."

"I know you. I know your car, your voice, your schedule. You get up early every morning and head to campus around eight, which must mean you like order and routine. You park in the same spot every day, which confirms my theory. You rarely have anyone over, so you're a bit of an introvert. There was one guy who used to show up, but I haven't seen him in six months."

The lonely cave inside her filled with hot mortification. She pressed her thumb against the edge of her ring and tried to act as though she wasn't flustered.

"You like to cook and you're damned good at it. My mouth waters every time I catch a whiff of whatever you're making. Happens almost every time I walk past your door." He raised an eyebrow. "Should I go on?"

"No. You've made your point." She regretted slapping the handcuff on him. This man was too observant, too smart. He wouldn't need much time to figure out she couldn't read some men. If Ivan had been mistreated by a therapist, he'd have a problem with any psychologist who wasn't at the top of her game. Who could blame him? A bad therapist could leave a serious bruise on someone's well-being, even someone as big and strong as Ivan.

He scowled at the chain stretched tight between their wrists. "I didn't expect this experiment to put me in handcuffs. Are there any other surprises I should know about?"

"This is the weirdest part of the experiment. I know being handcuffed is odd, but I'm confident we'll adapt to the situation."

"You're very optimistic, Doctor Garcia."

"Yes, I am. By the way, you can't call me 'Doctor' until I finish my internship. I've got three months of work to finish. In July, I'll finally become Doctor Garcia." This small talk was good. Maybe they'd find some common ground. "Where will you go after graduation?"

"Boston. I went to college there, so that place feels like home. Once I start my new job, I'll make enough money to have a life."

"I know what you mean. Living off a stipend isn't easy."

He nodded. "What about you? After your internship, where will you go?"

"Out west, hopefully. I want to live near the Rocky Mountains. I've applied to a few post-doctoral programs in Denver. I found one that specializes in self-reliance, which appeals to me. I want to learn everything I can to help young women be independent. If they can satisfy their own needs and wants, they'll be happier. Stronger."

The hard crease reappeared on his forehead. "Doesn't that go for men, too?"

"Yes, but I feel more comfortable working with women. I grew up in a family of females. I know the challenges they face. For many women, solitude is suspect. It's difficult to be self-sufficient if friends and family think you aren't whole unless you've got a boyfriend, a husband, or a family. This doesn't seem to be the case for men. When a guy is self-sufficient, he's respected for taking care of himself."

"Until he turns forty. After that, everyone thinks he should be married." A grin ghosted across Ivan's mouth. "That happened to my Uncle Bronislav. The day after his fortieth birthday, everyone in Slovokia tried to fix him up. He managed to stay single out of pure spite. Then he met Danika. Two weeks later, he married her."

"After only two weeks?"

"Every Antonov rushes to marry the one woman who believes the sum of his strengths is greater than the depth of his flaws." The corners of Ivan's eyes crinkled when he chuckled. "Now my uncle grumbles about being so happy."

"That's kind of adorable."

"And unnerving. No one is used to seeing him smile." Ivan nudged his glasses up the bridge of his nose. "You're right, though. Circumstances can be different for men and women, but we struggle with the same problems: fear, false preconceptions, unhealthy choices. If you offer a seminar on those topics, why can't men attend?"

"They can, but my seminars are designed specifically for women. I want them to take a close look at their beliefs and toss out the preconceptions that derail their goals. We delve into some very personal topics that are easier to discuss in small, same-sex groups." Tia reached for a biscochito, bit into it, and felt some grainy sands of sugar stick to her lip. She licked them off with a brief swipe of her tongue.

Ivan's gaze dropped to her mouth and jerked up again. "I still don't get it. Why can't men participate in these small discussion groups?"

"Because the women who attend these discussions need to figure out how to rely on themselves. I'm worried that if men participate in the seminar, they'll offer solutions."

"Now you're really confusing me. What's so bad about men trying to help?"

"Because the women in the program need to develop the confidence to rely on themselves. My mother is a good example of why this is important. She gave up her family, her friends, and her job to follow my father when he moved to Texas. To be honest, I think my father felt trapped. My mother couldn't find work, so he had to provide for her. After I was born, my father had two mouths to feed. That pressure got to him."

Ivan frowned. "Your father didn't want a family?"

"Right. Dad is an artist. He needs solitude to paint. Family life isn't for him, which is why he never married my mother and never spent much time with me. Eventually, he left for another woman, one who owned her own business and could stand on her own two feet. My mother couldn't. She depended on him for everything. When he left, she had nothing. I don't want other women to make the same mistake." Tia took another bite of the cookie. "Do you see what I mean?"

"I do and I don't." A cookie crumb landed on his thigh. He brushed it off with a quick swipe of his hand. "This campus is a place where we're supposed to encourage conversation, explore ideas, discuss problems. How can that happen if men can't participate, and vice versa?"

"I agree. Public discourse is important on campus. There's no better way to share ideas and broaden minds, but I'm here to help the women on campus identify the beliefs that set them up for dependency and failure. These feelings trigger behaviors that can be unique, terrifying, and intensely painful. The best way to treat these issues is within small groups or private counseling." There. No one could disagree with that, not even Ivan Antonov. She popped the rest of the biscochito into her mouth.

His gaze returned to her mouth and frowned again. "I have no idea what I was about to say."

"I know, right? Cookies are a huge distraction." She licked some sugar off her thumb.

"Right. Cookies." His nostrils flared on a deep inhale. "Very distracting."

Tia nudged the plate closer to Ivan. "Go ahead. Eat."

"Thanks." He grabbed a biscochito, took a bite, and did a double take at the uneaten half that remained in his fingers. "Good God, this is better than box tickets to a Bruins game." He shoved the rest of the cookie into his mouth. "Damn. These are off the hook. Do you want any more?" He tilted the plate toward her. "Grab some now, because they're gonna be gone in thirty seconds."

"Dig in, Mountain Man."

"Love it when you call me that." He balanced the plate on one hand and tucked into the cookies as though he hadn't eaten something sweet in months.

Tia sat back and watched, a little stunned he liked being

called Mountain Man. His hearty glee over something so simple as a bunch of biscochitos was kind of surprising, too.

He set the empty plate on the coffee table, chugged a few mouthfuls of water, and pointed a sharp look at her. "You kicked my ass at volleyball, dazed me with your honesty, and brought me to my knees with a plate of cookies. You've unearthed most of my weaknesses."

"Those are my weaknesses, too," she confessed. "I can't resist cookies, volleyball, and honesty. In fact, I should be completely honest and tell you that I played volleyball in college. So did the captain of The Freudian Slips."

"The tall, blond guy?"

"Yep. That's my friend, Wayne. He played for Stanford. Basically, your intramural team didn't have much of a shot at beating us."

"I already figured that out." He took one last swallow of water and set the empty bottle on top of the empty plate. "Congratulations, by the way. When you destroyed us, you won bragging rights and the league's cash prize. Good job."

"Thanks. It wasn't easy. You put up a good fight."

"Yeah, yeah. Whatever." He pointed to her. "You won, Miss Spike-a-lot. Would you like a moment to gloat?"

"Oh, I've gloated for the past twenty-four hours. I'm gloating right now. Every time I see you, I gloat." She drew a deep, satisfied breath and smiled. "Winning feels fantastic. Like happy birthdays, but with more chocolate frosting."

"All right, that's enough." He reached into his backpack.

"I should get to work."

"I'm still gloating."

"I know. I can see that little smirk of yours." He tugged a laptop onto his thighs.

Oh, no. She wasn't finished, yet. "Are you familiar with the French philosopher, Descartes? I believe he said, 'I gloat, therefore I am.'"

Ivan snorted. "Descartes said nothing of the sort."

"I'm also a fan of Julius Caesar, who said, 'Veni, vidi, gloatie.'"

Those bright eyes of his narrowed. "Gloating got Caesar into big trouble."

"And as the great Vince Lombardi would say, 'Gloating isn't everything, it's the only thing.'"

"Aaaaaand, this is when I ignore you." He opened the laptop with an abrupt move that dragged her hand onto the keyboard.

She jerked away, inadvertently yanking his hand onto her thigh.

"We should take off these handcuffs so I can type." He reached into his pocket.

"No, don't get your key. Removing the cuffs will invalidate our data. We can do this."

"Fine, then. You've got to get close." He grabbed her hand and tugged. "Get in my space, woman. We can't sit far apart like a couple of strangers on a bench."

"Geez, you get pushy when you've got a full stomach." But he seemed happier. His mouth had a relaxed tilt and his blue eyes sparkled. Tia wiggled an inch closer. "Better?"

"Nope. Get all up in my business."

"Your business had better let me get a book so I have something to read while you work." She snatched a textbook off of the coffee table and scooted until her thigh touched his. "Can you reach the keyboard now?"

"Yeah, that works for me. How about you?"

"This works for me, too." Not really. She was completely distracted by Ivan's hands, which were thick-boned and broad like the rest of him. Sure and strong, the type of man who made faded denim look as good as a black tux. His wide shoulders and thick arms were a fine example of what testosterone could build.

Now that she was plastered against him, a firm wall of heat radiated into her. All of that luscious warmth shrank the prickly goose bumps she'd tolerated all winter. For the first time in months, Tia didn't need the blanket she kept within reach of the couch. She. Was. Warm. With a man like Ivan around, a woman would save hundreds on her heating bill.

Not that she wanted him around or anything. A sweater would keep her just as toasty and wouldn't make her wonder if her self-sufficiency seminars should focus on men, too.

No. There were plenty of programs for men and not enough for women. She would stick to her goals. To that end, she opened her book and paged to the chapter on stress disorders. Over the past few months, she'd seen how self-doubt could trigger dependence, avoidance, and fear. Eager to find new ways to help women who were lonely and scared, Tia read until her eyes felt too dry to move across the page.

Fatigue pulsed through her. She closed her scratchy eyes for just a second and tilted. Her cheek landed on something dense and warm. Ivan's shoulder. He smelled like fresh air, toasted almonds, and silent promises.

The rapid tap of his fingers on the keyboard stopped.

She lifted her head and squinted at the fuzzy print on the page of her book.

"Hey." The word was a hoarse whisper near her ear.

A shiver danced along her scalp. She ignored the lovely feeling and turned a page to demonstrate she was awake. Not sleepy at all.

"I don't mind if you lean against me."

"Thanks, but I'm good." Because she'd stick to her plan. She'd pour all of her energy into her internship so she could finish her doctorate. After that, she'd find a post-doctoral job and eventually start her own private practice.

That's what a self-sufficient woman did. She stayed focused on her goals, even when she was with a thoughtful, hotter-than-a-habanero man who didn't mind if she leaned on him.

It was lonely, but worth the sacrifice.

CHAPTER FIVE

On a scale of ten, this dream was a twenty because everything felt so damned good. Soft couch cushions surrounded him. So did a warm woman. She snuggled up against him, the sweet curve of her thigh pressed against his throbbing cock. Ivan tilted his hips to increase the pressure and was rewarded with a sexy sigh against his skin. Delicate fingertips stroked his arm, the touch tender and affectionate.

With this woman, there was no guilt, no acrimony, no demands. Just pleasure. Happiness surged inside him, fusing all his broken wires.

He reached for more of her. A sharp prickle skidded up his forearm. Something pinched his wrist. He couldn't lift his right hand. The hazy edges of the dream splintered and he opened his eyes.

A bright ray of morning light slanted through the room, shocking evidence he'd slept past dawn. The sunlight fell on a row of precise vacuum tracks along a clean beige carpet. An empty plate sat near a neat stack of books on a coffee table.

Hot damn. He wasn't in his crappy apartment. He was somewhere much better, with Tia Garcia's bent leg pressed against his groin.

She'd fallen asleep with her head on his shoulder and her body cuddled against his side. The wavy ends of her brunette hair curled in loops across his chest like a signature on a deed. Sometime during the night, she'd dragged his hand—the one that was handcuffed— between her thighs.

What a great spot to land. He wanted to spread his fingers to explore the fascinating warmth between her legs, but that move would have to wait until she was awake. Fooling around with Tia would be a lot more fun if she knew what he was doing.

Her name came out of his throat in a husky abbreviation. "Tee."

She kept sleeping, unaware that the weight of her leg felt like an angel's wing against his devilish erection.

He shoved his glasses up the bridge of his nose and caught sight of her other hand resting on his forearm, her fingers lax and trusting. The morning light winked off her silver ring. Would that ring of hers feel cool against the hot skin of his dick?

Don't go there, you horny bastard. Have some class.

God, she felt better than a long summer day on the lake. He turned his head until his nose touched her hair. The glossy waves smelled like vanilla. He sank into a slow grin. "You're all up in my business."

"Shh." She patted his arm. "Don't drink the little duck."

"What duck?"

"In my teacup, near the thing."

He chuckled. "Honestly, I don't want to drink a little duck, whatever that is."

"El pato." She stretched.

The chain between pulled his hand closer to her groin. Ripe heat and soft fabric brushed against his knuckles. He wanted to slide a finger along that private hyperbola, plot the curve that led to her center, kiss her until she knew how much he ached for her. "Tia, you need to wake up. You've dragged my hand between your legs. Not that I'm complaining, but I thought you should know."

Her eyelids fluttered open. Dark irises pointed at him. She sat straight up, her spine as stiff as a copper pipe. "Oh, no. This is bad. We weren't supposed to spend all night together."

"All we did was sleep." And he felt brand new. Reborn.

"You've got to go." She yanked a small key out of her pocket to unlock her handcuff and his. The manacles fell in a loose heap between them. She stood and bumped into the coffee table.

He grabbed her forearm. "Whoa, you're not awake yet. Don't trip."

"I'm fine, really." She picked up his knapsack. "Here, this is yours."

"Thanks." He took the bag and rose, reaching around to make sure his wallet was still in his back pocket. The last time he looked, there were thirty-two bucks tucked inside. He wanted to spend every cent of that precious cash on her. "Want some breakfast? I know a place that makes killer waffles, the kind that are light on the inside and crisp on the outside. With toppings. Their hickory smoked bacon is stellar."

"Sounds tempting, but I'm not supposed to hang out with you. Not until tonight, like the experiment says. So get out of here, Mr. Waffles, and come back later." She tugged him toward the door.

He liked the feel of her hands on him. He got a kick out of how she shifted her grip to his upper arms to guide him across the threshold. He really enjoyed the brusque nudge on his lower back that pushed him into the hallway. A few inches lower, and her hands would land on his ass.

Oh hell, yes.

He pivoted. "You'll see me tonight?"

"Yes, for the last phase of the experiment. Check your email, okay? Annette sent a link to a survey that needs to be filled out by noon."

He flattened a hand on her door. "Will we have to wear handcuffs again?"

"No."

Damn. "Rope?"

"Nope." A long lock of chestnut hair fell over her eye. She looked half asleep and more delicious than bacon. "Leather? Lace? Licorice?"

"No, no, and definitely not licorice, but I appreciate the alliteration. Now go."

"I will when I get my boots." He tried to look annoyed but felt too damned content to scowl. "You've got a nice collection of boots lined up by your door, including mine. I doubt my size thirteen clodhoppers will fit you."

"Hm? Oh, right. Your boots. Sorry." She stuffed them into his arms. "Here. Bye."

"What about the duck?"

Her brown eyes squeezed into a bewildered squint. "What duck?"

"The one in your teacup."

"Oh, that." She laughed and tucked some wayward hair behind her ear. "I dreamt I cracked an egg and a tiny duck came out. He was a little thing, no bigger than an inch, so I let him swim in my cup of tea. How did you know?"

"You asked me not to drink the duck. Didn't make any sense, until now." He'd talk about ducks and teacups for the next two hours if that would keep the smile on Tia Garcia's face. "You have weird dreams."

"Yep." She poked him in the chest. "Back up, Mountain Man. Time to go."

He took a reluctant step back. "Figures. I finally meet someone who respects the parameters of scientific experimentation and she throws me out of her apartment."

"She'll let you back in at six o'clock." Tia closed the door.

Ivan wanted back in, wanted to spend the rest of the day with her. Saturdays were meant for something other than work, right? And being with Tia was damned fun. She spiked volleyballs at him, handcuffed him, called him funny things like Mr. Waffles, and gloated like a champ.

Yeah, he didn't like that she offered women-only

seminars, but he understood why she did. With any luck, he'd prove to her that men wanted to solve problems, not create them.

Right now, he had a big problem. He'd have to wait twelve hours until he could see Tia again. He was beginning to share her obsession with high-heeled boots, because those high heels and supple leather were the perfect accessory for her long legs.

He gave her door a soft goodbye tap. "See you later, Boots."

The overhead light near his apartment flickered like a sick strobe. Inside his place wasn't much better, but he'd grown accustomed to the stark emptiness. Having very little wasn't so bad. The simplicity of an uncluttered life appealed to him, but he did miss having a TV.

And steak. He missed steak.

If he wasn't careful about how much time he spent with Tia Garcia, he'd miss her more than rib-eye.

"Dial it back, Antonov. You're leaving here in six weeks. Eye on the prize." He placed his boots on the floor and pulled his laptop out of his bag. Might as well fill out the experiment's survey before he headed to the lab.

He sat at the wobbly old card table that was a poor excuse for a desk and checked his email. There were a few letters from the guys in his computer programming loop, the survey from Annette, and something from the law offices of Ingram and Goddard.

A thin lick of sweat sprung across his skin, as cold as a ghost's tongue. He stared at the subject line for a moment before he opened the email.

Dear Mr. Antonov,

The request to expunge your criminal record has been granted. All materials that relate to the restraining order filed against you have been destroyed, including police reports, records in the prosecutor's office, and court documents. In the near future, you will receive a certificate from the court to confirm that these records have been annulled. If the court or law enforcement agency is asked about your criminal record, the response will be: "No record exists."

You'll receive a copy of this letter via certified mail in a few days. Best wishes as you complete your job search.

Yours sincerely,
J. Goddard, Attorney at Law

His nightmare was finally over, but the shame would never go away. He had a past, something he wanted to hide. There was a good chance Tia might hear about the awful night that sparked his downfall. If she asked him to explain what happened, he'd have to admit he wasn't as smart as he was supposed to be, which sucked. Smart was all he had.

To preserve what little he had left of his reputation, he had to keep working hard. His accomplishments had to blaze brighter than the flames of his failure.

He answered Annette's survey, took a hot shower, and headed to the engineering quad. Campus was cold and quiet, a perfect time to get things done. He'd devote the next few hours to work on the presentation he'd give during his Phoros Technologies interview. With any luck, his innovative ideas to prolong battery life would win him a job in the city he loved.

Ready to work, he trudged up the wide marble steps of Harris Hall, swiped his ID against a sensor, and trotted upstairs to the third floor. The place was empty until he got to the robotics lab. That room was a pig sty, littered with junk because the guys who worked there were always dicking around. Today was no different. A makeshift goal teetered on a desk, testimony that very little work was getting done.

A tennis ball flew out of the room and smacked into Ivan's hip.

"Here we go again." He took a sharp left into the lab and held up the ball. "Who threw this?"

Four pairs of eyes landed on him. Three faces winced.

Eric Stanwick lifted a lacrosse stick with a negligent shrug. "I tossed that ball."

"Your bad toss almost flew into my lab," Ivan snarled between clenched teeth. "I've got three systems set up in there, and none of them can withstand a hit."

"Take a pill, Antonov. Nothing happened. We're just taking a break."

"Your type of break can destroy months of work. Stop screwing around." Ivan flung the ball into a trash can, tempted to whack the cocky sneer off Stanwick's round face. That dipstick didn't give a rip about destroying a research project that cost fifty-thousand dollars. Asshole.

"Sorry, Ivan." Bones, otherwise known as Jason, apologized.

"We weren't thinking." Smitty placed a lacrosse stick on a table and held up both hands.

Cosmo hid a tennis ball behind his back. "It won't happen again."

Yeah, right. Ivan strode across into the lab across the hall and tossed his backpack on a desk. "Stanwick is screwing around again."

Henry didn't look up from his laptop. "What's he playing this time? Baseball? Soccer?"

"Lacrosse. The fool recruited Bones, Smitty, and Cosmo to join in."

"If they destroy any lab equipment, they could lose their stipends."

"I just want Stanwick to lose that infernal smirk of his." Ivan removed his coat and felt a familiar twinge on his wrist. The biofeedback band had tightened during his walk across campus. "By the way, this device of yours shrinks in cold air."

"What? Let me see." Henry grabbed Ivan's wrist and tried to poke a finger under the wristband. "Shit, you're right. Why hasn't anyone else told me this?"

"Because I told the guys how to fix the problem. I'll show you." Ivan walked to the heating vent near the corner of the room and held his wrist under a steady stream of warm air. After a moment, the band's grip eased. "A little bit of heat does the trick."

"A low-tech fix for a high-tech problem. Good thinking. I'd better tell Annette about this." Henry resumed typing.

Ivan dropped into a chair. "What happens during the next phase of the experiment, Stretch?"

"You just have to hang out with Tia, that's all." Henry looked up from his screen. "Why? Is there a problem?"

"There's nothing wrong. I like Tia. A lot."

Henry opened his hands, palms up. "Then it's all good."

"For me, yeah. Not for her."

"Why not?"

"Because she's pursuing a doctorate in psychology so she can help women. If someone sees her with a guy who supposedly battered his girlfriend, people are gonna question Tia's judgment."

"Bullshit. You never hit your girlfriend." Henry's long neck turned a bright, angry red. "Why am I the only one who knows what happened?"

"I refuse to drag my ex through the mud. She got bad advice from an incompetent therapist and filed a restraining order because she didn't know what else to do."

"Stacy knew exactly what to do. When she realized you were smart enough to earn three patents that any computer engineering firm would pay good money to get, she knew you'd be able to support her in style. That plan got flushed down the toilet when you broke up with her, so she found the perfect way to punish you. She ruined your reputation and almost took everything you owned." Henry banged a fist against the desk. "That's not fair, dammit."

"It is fair. That's what I deserved for losing my temper

like I did." That temper rose again, but he tamped down the dangerous feeling because whenever he got angry, bad things happened. Those things had the power to corrupt everyone's opinion of him, and not even a registered letter from the Court would change their minds. "Some people think I'm bad news, Stretch. I don't want Tia to get any grief for hanging out with me."

"Stop punishing yourself. Eight months have passed since Stacy left. No one remembers what happened."

"I do." He recalled everything in vibrant, high-definition detail. The yelling, the rage, the heart-flattening desperation that had spewed out of him like acid. "I screwed up. Badly."

"Welcome to the club. I screw up every day." Henry reached for a bright orange box and opened the lid. "Have a donut."

"No, thanks." He knew better than to take one of Henry's favorite snacks. "I'll eat something, later."

"Eat something, now. You deserve a donut, because your numbers are off the charts."

"What numbers?"

"Your biofeedback measurements." Henry shoved a glazed donut into Ivan's hand and tapped a command on the laptop. "Look at this graph. We've plotted your pulse, skin temperature, and muscle tension levels on a scale of one to ten. During the beginning of the week, you operated at a steady stream of threes. You didn't feel much."

Ivan bit into the donut and gazed at the depressing straight line on the graph. "Looks like I have the emotional warmth of a robot."

"Nah, you remind me of a droid." Henry grinned. "With artificial intelligence."

Ivan snorted. "How does a droid like me help you?"

"Because your numbers had the most drastic change. I think your data is showing us what happiness looks like in real, measurable numbers. Here, look." Henry scrolled to a different graph. "Things got interesting when we played volleyball on Thursday. That's the first time your numbers shot up. Same thing happened last night. When you got close to Tia, your heart rate, respiration, and muscle tension readings exploded. You were a walking, talking firecracker all night. Very impressive. You were way beyond happy. Maybe even exultant. What does that look like on you? Did you actually smile?"

"Many times. I even flirted."

"Well, butter my butt and call me a biscuit." Henry leaned back and grinned. "Do tell."

"I asked Tia out for breakfast but struck out on that pitch. If I spend any more time with her, there's a good chance I'll ask her to—"

A loud crash boomed from across the hall.

Henry flinched. "That didn't sound good."

"I think we just heard a stipend break." Ivan tossed the donut back into the box and raced into the robotics lab. He skidded on some debris and almost landed on a motherboard. A decimated computer lay on the floor like a detonated bomb. Little bits of plastic, wires, and metal glittered on the linoleum tile. "What happened?"

Bones, Smitty, and Cosmo glanced at Stanwick, who

slumped against a desk and moaned.

Henry surveyed the destruction and shook his head. "This isn't good, fellas."

Ivan picked up a lacrosse stick, tempted to break the blasted thing in two. He'd told these screw-ups to stop dicking around and they hadn't listened. Now he'd have to fix everything, damn it, because he was the responsible one. The Brain. Always in charge, never at rest.

He slammed the stick onto a desk. "Someone had better start talking, *now*."

"We just wanted to toss the ball around before we got back to work," Bones admitted. "Working on the weekend sucks, but Dr. McNeil doesn't care about our time. He wants us to run his seminar even though we've got a huge computer architecture project to finish. All of this pressure is too much."

"Too much? McNeil is paying you to be here. This is your job, yet you treat this place like some dumpy playground." Ivan swung his arm toward the mess, which was everywhere. "Look at this place. There's garbage on every work surface, the floor is a disaster, and who thought it would be a good idea to put stickers on the ceiling? Hell, the only thing you haven't polluted is the trash can, which probably hasn't been used in weeks. If Dr. McNeil or the Dean of Engineering catches sight of this debacle, they'll think twice about funding your research next year. When are you going to grow up?"

Stanwick whimpered. "My arm hurts."

"Because you dove into a computer," Cosmo muttered.

Ivan took a second look at Stanwick. His forearm

was swollen and red. The arrogant prick had probably broken a bone. "Stretch, can you drive Stanwick to the infirmary?"

"Yeah, sure." Henry swung an impatient wave at Stanwick, who limped out of the room like a bird who'd just snapped a wing.

Bone's shoulders drooped. "Great. We'll never get this place ready for Dr. McNeil's seminar without Stanwick."

"Oh, come on. He wasn't that much help." Smitty chewed on his bottom lip like a kid who knew he didn't deserve any help. "Can you give us a hand, Ivan?"

"Give us your brain, too." Cosmo offered a hesitant smile. "I mean, if you have the time. You always get things done."

That part of his reputation was important to preserve. Ivan took another look at the floor and saw something scurry under a box. A mouse, probably. That thing looked well fed and lively. "When does this room have to be ready for the seminar?"

"Monday."

"That gives us two days to clean up. Bones, you take the first third of the room. Smitty, the middle is yours. Cosmo, focus on the rear third. Throw out every toy and piece of garbage you can find. While you do that, I'll catch the mouse I just saw."

"Good luck with that," Bones muttered. "He's been here for two months. No one can catch him. He's too smart."

"I wouldn't expect anything less from a critter who lives in our labs." His choice of words coaxed a smile from the group, which was a good sign. Cleaning up their mess wasn't how he meant to spend the weekend, but he wouldn't turn his back on these guys when they needed him. Somehow, he'd help them and find a way to show up at Tia's apartment by six. She was the only thing he looked forward to on his crappy agenda.

Smitty approached with an apologetic shrug. "Stanwick was supposed to edit the modules for Dr. McNeil's robotics seminar, but I'm not sure where they are."

"He might've uploaded a draft to the cloud. Check there." Ivan lifted an empty pizza box and found a clipboard with what looked like a petition clipped to the front. Signatures filled the front page. "What's this?"

"That belongs to Stanwick. He thinks you're right about groups like The Women's Grid, so he started a petition against any program that discriminates against men. He figured a document with real signatures would have more impact than an electronic version."

"True." Ivan scanned the first page of signatures and recognized a lot of names. Quite a few of his colleagues had decided to speak out against The Grid. This type of support was a surprise. For the first time in a long while, he wasn't the only one who wanted to shut down the group that vomited hate all over campus.

"Five hundred people signed in the past two days." Smitty said. "Everyone is mad about next week's seminar sponsored by The Grid. They're bringing in someone to talk about 'Toxic Masculinity.' No men allowed, of course."

"In other words, no man can defend himself if anyone in this so-called seminar says men are aggressive cretins." Ivan released a tight growl. "If toxic masculinity is a thing, so is poisonous femininity."

"Ha. Good one."

Ivan grabbed a pen. "I'm speaking to the Dean of Students again in a few days. If enough people sign this petition, the administration will feel a lot of pressure to defund The Grid and anything like it."

"Hell to the yeah. Any group that doesn't include men."

Damn. That meant Tia's program, too.

CHAPTER SIX

"It's okay, Pamela. I'm glad you called." A high-pitched whimper screeched into Tia's ear, followed by a sloppy sob. Something awful must've happened. Pamela never cried, not even when she spoke about her father's alcoholism or her mother's cruelty. "Take a deep breath and tell me what's going on."

"Greg came by my apartment last night. My roommates didn't want me to talk to him because of what he did a few weeks ago, but they agreed to let him see me if they could stick around. He didn't mind if everyone listened. He said how sorry he was for yelling at me. He said he'd do anything to make things right. He said he loved me." Pamela sucked in a watery breath. "And then he asked me to marry him."

Oh, no. Pamela hardly knew this man. They'd dated for three turbulent months until the relationship ended a short while ago. "How did you respond to his proposal?"

"I said yes! I love him, I really do." Her voice brightened. "He is graduating in May, and he wants me to come with him when he goes to law school. I can transfer my credits and finish my senior year wherever he ends up."

That's a terrible idea. Tia knew too many women who'd abandoned their goals to follow a man—like her mother—and when the relationship ended, the woman had nothing. The same thing could happen to Pamela. She might not be able to transfer all of her credits in order to get her degree. What a disaster. This girl was barely twenty, too young to make this rash decision work, but Tia fought hard to keep the judgment out of her voice. "Sounds like a lot has happened. How do you feel about getting engaged?"

"I don't know. My parents aren't happy. I wish they knew Greg like I do. You should see the ring he gave me. It's beautiful."

Support her. Keep her talking. "He must mean a great deal to you."

"Yes, he does. And he loves me. More than anyone else ever has." Pamela paused, her breath catching. "Mom and Dad don't want us to get married. I don't get it. Isn't getting married the right thing to do?"

Not if you hardly know the guy. Tia eluded Pamela's question with one of her own. "Have you and Greg set a date?"

"Greg wants to elope. He booked a flight to Las Vegas for tomorrow. I need to decide tonight, but I don't know what to do. I've always wanted a fairytale wedding with the white dress, flowers, and bridesmaids. Do you know what I mean?"

No, I don't. Fairytale weddings turned love into an event that cost too much and meant too little, which didn't appeal to Tia. Then again, she wasn't the one getting married. "Maybe you should tell Greg that you'd like a big wedding."

"Greg would rather save our money to buy a house. I see his point, but I don't know…" Pamela sniffled and blew her nose.

Two sharp knocks startled Tia. She glanced at the clock and realized it was almost six. Ivan was here, right on time. A little early, in fact.

Tia cradled the phone in her hand and opened the door.

Ivan stood in the hallway, a mountain of a man with bright, intelligent eyes. This time, he wasn't wearing glasses. Without those studious frames, he looked more intense. His fierce good looks made Tia's pulse pound in spots she shouldn't acknowledge, especially while she was dealing with a crisis.

She pointed to the phone to indicate she was on a call, waved him inside, and resumed speaking to Pamela. "Do you need to talk some more? We could meet at the Counseling Center."

"No, not there. If one of Greg's friends see me going in there, they'll tell him I'm upset."

"How about the Campus Café?"

"Too crowded. No privacy." Pamela sniffled again. "Never mind. I'll be okay."

"You'll definitely be okay, but right now you sound

a little sad." Tia rubbed her thumb against her ring and tried to ascertain whether Pam might do something rash, like elope. "Do you feel like meeting me in front of the library? We can talk while we take a walk."

"It's really cold tonight."

"Right. The weather isn't good." Now what? Finding a private, warm place to meet wasn't easy if the Counseling Center wasn't an option.

Ivan touched Tia's arm. "Use my office in Harris Hall."

That offer was unexpected. Helpful, too. She nodded and spoke to Pamela. "We can use an office in the engineering quad. Can you meet me in front of Harris Hall? Great. See you in thirty minutes." She ended the call and gave Ivan a grateful smile. "Thanks for your help. I'm afraid I have to work for a little while."

"No problem. I've got a few things to do in the lab."

"I'll grab my coat so we can go."

"Hold on, I want to give something to you." He pulled a small brown paper bag out of his coat pocket. "Here. This is to thank you for feeding me last night."

Not sure what to expect, she peered inside the bag. "A teacup? Wait, there's a little duck, too."

"Like your dream."

"Very much so." She lifted the gift out of the bag and grinned at the rubber duck that sat inside the teacup. "I like the blue flowers around the rim."

"I figured blue was a good bet, considering you've got a blue pottery on your shelves and blue curtains on your windows."

This man really did pay attention. Carefully, Tia set

the teacup on the coffee table so she'd see the pretty piece of china every time she sat on her couch. "I love it. Thank you, Ivan."

"I need to add more thing." He tugged a plastic bottle out of his other pocket and poured some water into the teacup until the little duck bobbed in the center. "There. He's swimming, now. Good stuff, huh?"

His broad smile revealed a row of straight, white teeth. Two dents that could've been dimples appeared within his beard on either side of his mouth. Good humor and pleasure beamed from his bright eyes, a sign Ivan was one of those people who genuinely enjoyed the act of giving.

Tia pressed a hand against her fluttery stomach, surprised to get such a sweet present from a man who looked like he could crush a teacup in the palm of his hand. Perhaps last night had changed things. Maybe he'd discovered that all psychologists weren't bad. She hoped he'd found something to like about her, because she'd discovered plenty of things to like about him.

He was thoughtful. Funny. Warm. He loved food but didn't seem to eat enough. And he went out of his way to say thank you.

She almost gave him a hug, but remembered the way he balked the last time she'd embraced him. She reached for her coat, instead. "Ready to go?"

"Bring your courage. You're about to ride in Sturdy Stella. She's a Ford Galaxy 500, with original bench seats and a V-8 engine. Even though she's over fifty years old, don't call her an antique. She's more like a hurricane on steroids."

"I'm intrigued and somewhat terrified." Tia buttoned her coat and followed Ivan out of the apartment. Her boot heels made a pleasant tap against the floor as she trotted downstairs beside him. "I don't mean to question your plan, but won't we get to Harris Hall faster on foot?"

"Yes, but I need to drive into town to pick up some pizza for you, me, and the guys in the lab." He opened the lobby door for her and squinted at the small icy pellets that fell from the charcoal sky. "A night like this needs melted cheese on soft bread."

"Wise words." Tia pulled on her mittens as they walked into the parking lot. "Did you park next to my car?"

"Where else would I park?" Ivan grinned at her.

She grinned, too.

He opened the passenger door and lifted one dark eyebrow. "Sturdy Stella needs a new muffler, so this'll be a loud ride. Ready?"

"As I'll ever be." Tia settled onto the passenger seat. The car's interior was spotless. There wasn't a fleck of dirt or a wayward receipt anywhere. She might need to add "neat freak" to her assessment of Ivan Antonov.

He slid behind the steering wheel and fired up the engine. The muffler's loud growl prevented much discussion during the short ride into town. When Ivan parked by the curb and pulled the key out of the ignition, the engine backfired.

An elderly couple jerked to a halt on the sidewalk. The old man glared.

Ivan rolled down the window and spoke to them. "Sorry about the noise. My car sounds awful but she's got a big heart."

The old man's eyebrows wiggled like two gray caterpillars as he scanned the sedan's long, powerful body. "What is she? A sixty-seven?"

"A sixty-six." Ivan tapped the steering wheel. "She never gives up."

"Hold on to her. She'll give you a great ride." The old man's mouth split into a gap-toothed grin. He grabbed the elbow of the old woman and resumed walking.

"Geesh." Tia made a face at Ivan. "A great ride?"

"Did that sound dirty to you, too?"

"Definitely."

"I'll be damned." He watched the old couple totter away. "When I saw him jump, I thought he was about to have a heart attack."

Tia shook her head. "I think that man's heart, and other things, work just fine."

"Good for him."

"Good for her."

Ivan laughed and reached for the handle on his door. "Do you want to tag along with me, or stay in the warm car?"

"I'll go with you. I love this place." She accompanied him into Lotza Pizza. The line at the pick-up counter was fairly long, but Tia didn't mind. A bright fire roared inside the restaurant's signature brick oven and the yeasty scent of fresh dough made her mouth water. A sudden, sharp pain diminished her pleasure. She removed her mittens and plucked at the too-tight yellow biofeedback device around her wrist. "This wristband shrinks whenever I'm out in the cold air."

"Yeah, mine too. Heat will loosen the band. Here, let me fix the problem." Ivan curled his warm hand around her wrist, his thick fingers gentle. "This should work."

Boy, did it. Not only did the band loosen, so did her limbs. Her knees wobbled like gelatin and her arms went slack, but she reminded herself this wasn't a date. This was the last phase of the experiment. After tonight, she might not spend time with Ivan again. Saddened by that notion, Tia turned her head and caught sight of a pretty woman with long blonde hair, lips dipped in nude gloss, and a perfect nose.

Taryn Kendrick. She was seated at a table near the wall, alone. Or maybe not. She could be waiting for someone. Someone like Mason Kendrick.

This might not end well.

Facing an ugly situation was nothing new to Tia, but this was the first time she was in the same room with The Wife.

There was a good chance Taryn had never discovered that her husband was unfaithful. Or maybe she had. Married people could sense when their spouse was dating someone, right? After all, Mason possessed a face that was easy to read.

Tia could see the want and the happiness in his expression whenever he was near, yet she hadn't seen the most important thing. He was married. He had a daughter, too, one who was seven years old, close to the age Tia had been when her father left for another woman.

Guilt pierced her with long, thin fangs. She pulled

out of Ivan's hold and unbuttoned the collar of her coat, trembling with a sickening combination of mortified heat and contrite cold.

Ivan looked over his shoulder at her. "Do you want something to drink?"

"Hm? N-no." Her stomach rolled. She pressed a hand against her midsection, but the firm pressure of her palm magnified a sudden clench of anxiety.

He tugged the wallet out of his back pocket and paused. "You okay?"

"No. I'll meet you outside." She hurried out to Ivan's car. Thankfully, he hadn't locked the doors. She ducked inside and sank into the lumpy comfort of Sturdy Stella's wide bench seat.

A minute later, Ivan strode out of the restaurant. He placed two boxes of pizza in the back seat, slid into the front seat, and moved all the way toward Tia to loop an arm around her shoulders. "You're shaking. I need to know what's wrong."

"I saw someone I didn't expect to see." Another shiver rattled through her. She leaned into Ivan's solid side, grateful for his warmth. "I panicked."

He cupped his hand around her shoulder. "I love the way you tell me things. I never have to guess with you. Please keep talking."

"When I started my internship a few months ago, I filled in for a colleague who counseled patients at the hospital. While I was there, I met a doctor. He flirted with me and I enjoyed the attention. Eventually, we went out on a few dates." She stared at the thin layer of snowflakes that had begun to cling to the windshield. "He's the man you noticed at my apartment a few months ago."

"Dark hair. Expensive suit. Shiny shoes." Ivan gave a terse nod. "I remember."

"We went out to dinner a few times. A week after our third date, I saw him with another woman at the grocery store. They were using the same cart. It was the first time I saw a ring on his finger."

"He was married?"

"Yes. For ten years. They were laughing in the dairy aisle, which surprised me. Yogurt isn't that funny." She inhaled, not quite able to fill her lungs. "I didn't want to make a scene near the cottage cheese, so I walked away. He saw me, though, and later that night he called to say he'd separated from his wife but they were living in the same house. According to him, their split was friendly for the sake of their daughter."

"Breakups are never friendly."

"When I saw his wife a minute ago, I didn't know how to react. I couldn't apologize to her because she doesn't know me. She has no idea I went out to dinner with her husband. I kissed him, too." Ashamed by the memory of that lusty kiss, Tia pulled on her mittens. Her clammy palms stuck to the yarn. "He lied to me. Even though I know he misled me, I feel guilty. If I'd known he was married, I never would've gone near him."

"I know." Ivan tucked her closer. His fingers curled into the fabric of her coat. "That guy deceived you and his wife. He's got the morals of a snake."

"He has a daughter, which makes matters worse.

She will be crushed if he leaves. I know, because I was a little girl when my father took off." Tia paused for a moment, remembering that soul-deep confusion when she was a kid. "I swore I'd never be someone who'd break up a family. But a few months ago, I became The Other Woman. I hate that. Makes me feel like a fraud. That's why I panicked in the pizzeria."

Ivan pulled back an inch to look at her. "Are you always this open?"

"I try to be. Over the past four years, I've learned that honesty heals. Thanks for letting me vent." Opening up felt good, but she felt vulnerable after revealing her dumb mistake. Embarrassed, too. She never had a clue Mason lied to her. Around here, he was probably the easiest guy to read. Not like Ivan, with his fierce eyes and feral frown that confused her.

In fact, he looked mighty fierce and feral right now.

She scooted out of his warm hold and buckled up. "We'd better get going. I need to meet someone and you've got pizza to deliver."

"That can wait." His furry jaw jutted forward. "I'm not starting this car until you're fine."

"I'm fine. Really." But her heart thumped and her nose stung as his sharp gaze stayed on hers. She stared back.

"You sure?" He put his hand on hers. "You're good?"

The warmth of his palm knitted into her mitten. Her knuckles tingled under the firm pressure of his hold, almost as though every joint in her hand knew this man was concerned about her. Judging by the angry slant of his eyebrows, Ivan wanted to track Mason down and deliver some justice on her behalf. At least, that's what her instincts believed. Her brain wasn't so sure.

My father didn't care about me. Why would any other man?

A psychologist with Daddy issues. Tia hated being such a cliché. She pulled out of Ivan's grip and nodded. "I'm good."

"Fine, then. Let's go." Ivan reached for his keys and started the engine.

By the time they parked near the engineering quad, the car smelled like warm cardboard and melted cheese. Ivan picked up the pizza boxes and jerked his head toward the cluster of brick buildings. "I know a shortcut."

Tia trailed behind him, which gave her a front row view of how the back pockets of his jeans cupped his butt. With every step he took, denim stretched across firm, round cheeks. The sight was kind of hypnotic. He definitely had the ass of a Mountain Man, with two hard globes that looked strong enough to climb the steepest trail. That butt was probably warm, too. Maybe a little furry, too. The perfect thing to fondle on a cold night.

She skidded on a patch of snow and decided staring at Ivan Antonov's ass wasn't a smart thing to do in nasty weather, so she yanked her gaze to the impressive brick buildings that surrounded the engineering quad. A slender young woman sat on Harris Hall's stone steps. Her small form was hunched over and small.

Tia rushed over to place a hand on the girl's shoulder. "Pamela?"

She lifted her head. Her eyes were puffy and red. Tears

had washed away most of her makeup, leaving her skin blotchy. She sniffled and saw Ivan. "Who's he?"

"A friend of mine," Tia said, noticing a dark, purple smudge below Pamela's eye. Was that a bruise? Had someone hit her? Worried by that awful possibility, Tia cupped Pamela's narrow elbow, anxious to get her somewhere warm and safe. "Let's go inside."

She guided her toward Ivan, who pressed his wallet against a sensor and held open the door for them. With long, purposeful strides, he led them up three flights of stairs that smelled like plastic. He brought them into a room that contained two desks, a bunch of computer equipment, and a tall mechanical thing that had two steel hands and an eerie metal head.

Ivan flicked on the lights. "Sit at my desk right here. Take as long as you need. I'll be across the hall if you need anything."

Tia thanked him and guided Pamela into a chair. "Tell me what's going on."

"Greg keeps texting me. He wants to know if I'm going to Vegas with him. He really wants to get married." Pamela wiped her eyes and hiccupped. "He says I shouldn't leave him for making one mistake. He wants me to forgive him for what happened at that party. I think I can, because I know he wasn't himself."

"Wait, I'm missing something. I remember that you broke up with him after he yelled at you during a party. What else happened?"

"I was talking to a guy. Greg thought he was bothering me. The two of them got into a yelling match. I told Greg to back off, but he punched the guy and started a big brawl."

Brawls were never good. Guys who started them weren't, either. "Does Greg get physical when he loses his temper?"

"Just that once. He'd had way too much to drink. He was wasted." Pamela seemed too willing to excuse Greg's boozy behavior, perhaps because she'd grown up with a father who drank too much.

Was this girl willing to excuse a man for hitting someone, too? Tia had to find out. "Has Greg ever hit you?"

Pamela paled. "He'd never do that."

"Your eye looks bruised. If someone hit you, that's not right."

"No one hit me, I swear. The dark circles under my eyes are from a bad a sinus infection, that's all. I'd never be with a man who hurt me." Pamela's eyes widened in horror at the thought. Her body language was open, her expression earnest and her torso pointed directly at Tia, all signs that she was telling the honest truth.

Tia offered an encouraging nod. "Okay. What happened after the fight at the fraternity?"

"I told Greg I didn't want to see him any more because he'd frightened me. I was so upset, I even told my parents. That was a mistake. I shouldn't have said a thing. Now they don't want me to see him, ever." Pamela pulled a tissue out of her pocket and blew her nose. "Greg has changed. He's not drinking anymore, he's not taking anything either. He's been clean ever since we broke up, and he promises to stay that way, but my parents don't believe him. They won't pay my tuition if I transfer to be with him, but I want to be with him so much, it hurts."

That agony was evident on her face, proof that love hurt. Tia could relate. Every time she fell in love, pain followed. "You must feel like no matter what you decide, you'll upset someone you care about."

"Yes." Pamela cried. "That's exactly how I feel."

They spoke for over an hour. Pamela decided not to elope, but stay engaged. She seemed calmer when she left.

Tia felt worse. Her stomach was a tight knot and she could barely summon the energy to stand. This impromptu counseling session had taken a lot out of her, mostly because she wasn't entirely sure the dark mark under Pamela's eye was from a sinus infection. If Greg had hit someone at a frat party in anger, there was a frightening possibility he'd hit his girlfriend.

However, frightening possibilities weren't reality. She had to trust her instincts, and everything inside her believed that Pamela was telling the truth. Reading women was easy for her. If only she could read men just as well.

Like Ivan. Tia paused to gaze at his desk. No notepads, no books, no pens littered the surface. Either he was a major neat-freak, or he'd purged his work area because he was a few weeks from graduation. He seemed willing to get by with very few resources, including a beat-up knapsack that had a rip along the zipper, the pair of faded jeans he usually wore, an empty desk, and a car that literally screamed for a tune-up. Ivan seemed to live on less than every other graduate student on campus.

She turned off the overhead light and walked across the hall to another lab. Ivan was alone in the spacious room, hunched over an open computer. Always working, this man.

He looked up from a tangle of wires. "How'd things go?"

Tia thought of Pamela's tremulous smile when she'd decided to remain in Vermont to finish her degree. "Everything is okay."

"Is it? Looked like someone hit her."

Of course he'd notice. Nothing got by Ivan. Tia shook her head. "I'm sorry. I can't talk about what's going on in her life."

"Client confidentiality, right? Fine, I understand." He placed a pair of pliers in a small toolbox and studied her. "Most people can talk to their friends when they have a tough day at work. You can't. That must not be easy."

"I can turn to one of the psychologists in my group whenever I need help." She needed help, now. Her knees felt like two wobbly bowls of gelatin whenever Ivan acted like she mattered. Would he treat her this well when he discovered that her next seminar was another women-only event?

Maybe not. She hadn't done a thorough job of convincing him why those seminars were important, but the night was still young.

She pulled a hand through her hair and forced a smile. "Want to hang out with Annette and Henry? They're watching TV in his apartment."

"Hell, no." His intense gaze took a slow trip from her eyes all the way down to her feet. "I've got other plans for you, Boots."

Chapter Seven

Ivan drove the blunt edge of his fingernails into the meat of his palm. His wonky knuckle popped. A bolt of pain shot through his hand. One glance at Tia's long legs in those leather boots and he'd gone all toxic male on her.

Hell, no. I've got other plans for you, Boots.

Instead of letting his inner caveman out, he should've told her that he just wanted to be with her. He'd thought about her all day, and not just about how great she looked or how good she felt beside him. He liked the lighthearted way she teased him, the quiet way she listened to him, the honest way she spoke to him. Now that she was finally within reach, he wanted to yank her into his arms for a deep kiss. As soon as his mouth touched hers, maybe she'd strip off that clingy white sweater and beg him to take her.

In his dreams.

Instead, she paused by one of the tables and gave him

a puzzled look. At least she didn't bolt, which is what she usually did whenever they ended up in the same room. This goofy experiment must've eased some of Tia's hesitance. Over the past two days, she'd talked to him more than she ever had. Last night, she'd cuddled up to him and now he could barely contain his need for more. This craving had turned him into something out of the Cro-Magnon period, ready to pound his hairy chest and howl.

Somewhere beneath all this raging testosterone, he had a brain. Might be a good time to use that organ rather than the long one pressed against the zipper of his jeans.

He retrieved one of the pizza boxes and opened the lid. "I saved two slices for you. Figured you might be hungry."

"I'm starving." She grabbed a slice and took a bite. "Ohmygah, thisizmazing."

Even when she had a mouthful of cheese, this woman was adorable. He grinned at her and reluctantly dragged his attention back to the computer he'd been rewiring.

Tia sank in a chair and looked around. "Is this your lab?"

"No. I do most of my work in the room you were just in. Another grad student runs this lab, but he broke his arm this morning. I stepped in to help his group prepare for a seminar. They needed a hand to get everything done. We're halfway there."

"Where are they now?"

"They went home after they finished cleaning the lab."

She pointed her slice of pizza at the motherboard he'd just installed. "Why didn't someone stick around to help you?"

"Because I can reassemble these components faster than anyone else." If he worked hard enough, he might restore his good name before he left campus.

Tia took another bite of pizza and chewed for a moment. "Doesn't seem fair you're the only one working late on a Saturday night."

"I'm used to working late."

"Still doesn't make it right." She tossed her crust into the box and took the other slice. "Just because you can do something faster or better shouldn't mean you have to do everyone's work."

"Last I checked, working hard was an admirable thing to do." And he wasn't going to stop busting his ass, even if he resented the way some people dumped a shit-ton of work on him. Bones and Smitty and Stanwick seemed to think he had nothing better to do, which was damned close to the truth. He'd practically lived in the lab for the past two years because his private life contained nothing but loneliness, and why the hell was he thinking about this now?

Must be Tia. She was the only one who thought he worked too much.

Ivan grabbed the uneaten crust she'd discarded, unwilling to let a perfectly good chunk of bread go to waste. Took him one bite to realize Tia's lips had just been on the food he was chewing. Suddenly, eating her discarded crust became an erotic thing, almost as personal as a kiss. She was inside his mouth, now. *God.*

Heat filled the shells of his ears, which burned like a

couple of hot diodes on an overloaded circuit. His heart pounded, pumping life into his groin. He was getting a hard-on from the simple act of finishing Tia Garcia's food, which kind of made sense. He hadn't had good food, or sex, for over a year.

Seemed like whenever Tia was around, his stomach felt too empty and his cock felt too needy. Emptiness, he could deal with. But need? That rattled him.

He closed the computer with a sharp shove. Manipulating a screw to fit into the small hole on the computer's side wasn't easy with two shaky hands, but he succeeded and kept going. A screw in the right corner, the left corner. One in the upper corner and damn, he was missing one. Where was the stupid ass screw?

"Ivan."

The quiet way she said his name made his ears blaze hotter. Dark, fierce energy filled him. He reached for a screwdriver and caught the scent of her. Like cookies. His hands tingled with the urge to stroke her skin. His lips remembered the taste of her mouth, soft and sweet. He didn't dare look at her, but his peripheral vision grew so sharp, he could pinpoint the exact spot where her sweater clung to the curve of her breast.

"Ivan?"

"*What?*"

"Here." Tia placed another crust in his hand. "You can have this, too."

"Uh, thanks."

"You're the one who deserves thanks. I'm glad you saved some dinner for me. I needed the food." She gave his forearm a brief squeeze and stood. "I'll toss the empty pizza boxes into the trash bins in the hallway. Otherwise, this room will smell like cheesy cardboard in the morning."

That wouldn't be good, especially if Dr. McNeil happened to stop by to check if the lab was ready for his seminar. Before Ivan could get his ass in gear to help clear away the remnants of dinner, Tia carried both boxes out of the room and even nabbed an empty water bottle someone had missed.

Damn. He couldn't remember the last time someone helped him around here. This lab wasn't hers. She'd probably never set foot here again, yet she treated the robotics room as though the space was important. The way she treated people. The same way she treated him.

He felt a pang in his gut had nothing to do with hunger. Sliding into a chair, he ate the last bit of pizza crust as he stared at the empty doorway. No one was around, which made sense. It was Saturday evening. Most people were hanging out with friends or sprawled in front of a television with a cold beer.

Not him. Weekends were the best time to get work done. Alone, with no interruptions. Nothing but him and the dismal feeling that he'd never fix his broken reputation.

The sound of boot heels against the hallway's hard floor eased the brittle tension along the back of Ivan's neck. Tonight, he wasn't alone. Tia Garcia was here, and she was walking right toward him.

She entered the lab and paused by a small stack of

boxes. "Want me to throw these away, too?"

"No, thanks. Let's not work anymore. Want to take a walk?"

"I'd like that."

After retrieving their coats and locking up, they headed outside. For the first time in days, the snow had stopped falling. A peaceful quiet blanketed campus. Ivan strode along the sidewalk that led into town and glanced at Tia, struck by her beauty. She belonged on some beach in a bikini, not hidden away in the cold mountains of Vermont. "How'd you end up here at Albrecht University?"

"I liked the program and the mountains. This place is much prettier than my flat hometown in Texas."

"You mentioned that you grew up with women. Were they sisters?"

"Friends. My mother and I lived with another single mother and her two daughters after my father left." She tucked a long dark curl behind her ear and smiled. "There was lots of estrogen in our apartment."

"I can relate, in a way. There was lots of testosterone in my house. I grew up with two brothers. Us boys were always breaking something. By mistake, not on purpose." He shrugged. "With three big kids in a small house, things got knocked over. Including me, since I was the shortest of the bunch."

Her gaze traveled up the length of him. "I can't picture you as the smallest one in the family."

"I'm only six foot two. Gabe is an inch taller and Victor is a beast. He could've played professional football." Ivan lengthened his stride as though walking faster would propel him from the sacrifices Victor had to make for him.

The residential quad contained a lot more activity than the academic quad. A bunch of students played football in the snow in front of a rowdy crowd. Ivan stepped in front of Tia to cut a path through a knot of frat boys.

Once he reached a clear spot, Ivan picked up the conversation. "Is your mom still in Texas?"

No Tia.

He slammed on the brakes and looked over his shoulder. She stood a few feet away, staring at a series of hand-made signs stuck into the snow.

END WOMEN-ONLY SEMINARS!

IF YOU KEEP MEN OUT OF A CONVERSATION, IT'S NOT A CONVERSATION.

LET DICKS IN.

BUST WALLS, NOT BALLS.

IF TOXIC MASCULINITY IS A THING, SO IS POISONOUS FEMININITY.

Shit. Someone had plastered his words on a crappy poster. Regret gathered in the back of his throat like phlegm, thick and tough to swallow.

Tia turned toward him, her face a pale oval within the wavy length of her dark hair. "This isn't good. I'm not trying to alienate men. I'm trying to empower women who need help."

Gutted by the hurt on her face, he tried to explain. "A lot of men want to be part of the solution. Why not let us participate?"

"Because some topics are difficult to discuss in mixed company."

"I disagree. Men and women can talk about anything."

"Yes, if there's a decent amount of trust among a group of men and women, they can talk about anything." She notched both hands on her hips. "There are some problems that need to be treated with special care."

"Like what?"

"Like sex."

He laughed. "If you think men don't want to talk about sex, you're dead wrong."

She rolled her eyes. "I counsel a lot of women who don't want to talk about sex."

"Are you kidding me?"

"I'm serious. That topic is difficult to discuss."

"I'm not convinced. Give me an example." He spread his arms and opened his hands wide enough to feel the cold March air chew on his fingers. "What, exactly, can't women discuss in front of men?"

"Climax. Orgasm. Coming. The Big O." She glared at him. "In other words, how to rub one out."

Hearing those words tumble out of that mouth pulled the plug on his train of thought. His brain crashed like a computer with a bad hard drive. Took him a minute to boot back up. He was tempted to ask her to repeat herself just so he could hear her say *rub one out* again, but that was a hellaciously bad idea. If he wanted to prove that men could talk about sex in a reasonable fashion, he couldn't act like a frigging fifth grader.

"If some women are embarrassed to admit they're having trouble reaching a climax, they're in good company," he said. "A ton of men are embarrassed to admit that they don't know what they're doing in bed. If you offer a seminar on the art of female climax, book the largest room on campus. You might as well use the football stadium, because every guy I know would give his left arm to learn how to please his woman." Even as the words left his mouth, Ivan knew some jerks would attend the seminar just to hear women talk about sex.

Tia balled her hands. "This isn't just about figuring out how to climax during intercourse. You'd be surprised by the number of women who don't know what a climax feels like. For them, that's incredibly difficult to admit."

"Difficult doesn't mean impossible."

"Okay, let's turn things around. Would a man be able to talk about a sexual problem if he knew some women were listening? What if he didn't know most of these women? What if he had no idea whether these strangers would gossip about him after the session? What if one of them might be someone he'd like to date?" Tia poked his chest. "Do you really believe a friend of yours would want to confess that every once in a while, he has trouble holding an erection?"

"That would be painful to admit, but that doesn't mean we should ban members of the opposite sex from uncomfortable discussions." He leaned toward her, liking the soft pressure of her mitten against his coat. "What happened to your 'we can do this' attitude? Why can't you figure out some way to include men in these conversations, even the difficult ones?"

"Because I'm dealing with people who write horrible things like this." She waved her hand toward the LET DICKS IN sign. "The guy who wrote this sign might treat a seminar on female sexuality like a joke. I have to protect the individuals who are so desperate to change, they're willing to seek help, which is why I'm running programs for women. And yes, another intern is offering programs for men. By and large, the Counseling Center offers coed seminars on most topics, but some sensitive discussions are best handled within same-sex groups."

"You're setting a dangerous precedent, Tia. This campus is supposed to be a place that supports the exchange of ideas for everyone to hear. If the administration says you can exclude me from your seminars, then groups like The Women's Grid can exclude me from their speakers, who routinely bash men. According to them, all guys are sadistic brutes who want to marginalize women. If I can't hear those accusations, how the hell can I defend myself from them?"

"I don't know. I'm at a loss." She took another look at the signs and her shoulders drooped. "People are starting to throw insults, which is only going to hurt feelings and create more strife. In an atmosphere like this, no one wins."

"True." But he felt like he'd won something big, because

he'd just found someone who didn't stoop to insults or guilt during a fight. This woman was gold. "This might sound odd, but I enjoy arguing with you. You make me think. You're willing to discuss our differences in a benevolent way. And you never get spiteful when we are at odds. Thanks for all that."

Her eyes went wide with surprise. Then, she grinned. "Right back 'atcha."

"Want to get off campus? A walk into town might do us some good." He nudged her arm. "Trust me, Boots."

She threw a wistful look toward the golden glow created by the bright lamps along Main Street. "I haven't been in town for a while."

"Because you've been working too hard. Like me. We both need a break." He tucked his hands into his pockets and offered his elbow. "I'll show you where I found your duck."

"This, I've got to see." She tucked her hand in the crook of his arm. "Show me where you got the teacup, too."

"Deal." Loving the feel of her mitten on his coat sleeve, he led her to the antique shop where he'd found the teacup. A few doors down, he showed her the toy store where he'd found the duck. None of the shops were open this late on a Saturday night, so Tia peered into the storefront windows and he admired her reflection in the glass. They meandered all the way down Main Street until they got to the off-campus movie theater.

Ivan glanced up at the brightly lit marquee. "Want to catch a flick?"

Tia craned her neck to see what was playing. "I've

never heard of this movie."

"Me neither. Who knows, the film might be good." He reached for his wallet.

Tia darted in front of him and slid her debit card through the slot in the ticket booth.

He grabbed her elbow. "What are you doing?"

"Getting tickets." She offered him one. "You bought dinner. This is on me."

"No, Tia. I brought you here. I'll pay."

"It's completely unfair to make you pay for everything." She tucked the ticket into his ratty coat pocket and walked into the busy lobby.

Not used to being with a self-sufficient woman who paid her own way, he stalked after her. "When the heck are you gonna let me pay for the stuff I'm responsible for, like the dent in your car? You have no idea how this is eating at me."

"Oh, I have a pretty good idea." She headed for the concession stand. "Want some popcorn?"

"Yeah, and I'm buying." Gah, he was going Cro-Magnon again. He could feel the imaginary animal skins chafing his back. He shoved a ten toward the kid behind the counter. "One large bucket and two waters."

Armed with enough popcorn to feed ten computer engineers, Ivan led the way into the dim theater and felt her behind him, close enough that the front of her wool coat swooshed against the back of his nylon jacket, his new favorite sound.

He paused by a row of seats. "Want to sit here?"

"Okay." She settled into the seat beside him and

unbuttoned her coat. "Ivan, I—"

"Listen, there's—"

They both paused and gestured for the other to continue.

"You go first," he insisted, determined to be a gentleman.

"There's something you should know. Remember the married guy I told you about? He always tried to keep me in his debt. At first, he wanted to fix the blouse he'd spilled juice on, so he bought me a new one. Then he wanted to buy me dinner. He even tried to upgrade my cell phone. Whenever he did those things, I felt like he didn't believe I could take care of myself. He wanted to pay for everything so I'd have trouble leaving if I discovered his lies." Tia paused and took a breath. "I'm struggling to trust again. If you can give me a little time to get used to the idea that you want to fix what you broke, I'll give you the chance to pay for my car repair."

There was that honesty, again. Surprised him, every time. "Hey, no problem. I can adapt. Your car, your rules."

"Thanks." She relaxed and ran her fingers through her hair.

Good lord, she could've been cast in a shampoo advertisement. Glossy hair cascaded down past her shoulders in loose waves that framed a gorgeous face. Thanks to the simple pair of black jeans and plain white sweater she wore, she looked approachable. The type of woman who liked ducks and teacups and pizza. He tilted the bucket of popcorn to lure her close.

She crammed some kernels into her mouth. "Oh,

wow. You got butter on this. You really know how to treat a girl."

"In a few weeks, I'll be able to afford a lot more than buttered popcorn." But buttered popcorn tasted like steak when he was with her.

"Do you have a job lined up in Boston?" she asked.

"I've got offers from various firms, but I want to work for Phoros Technologies. I have an interview with them next Wednesday. They design state-of-the-art computer parts, which is what I want to do. The woman who founded Phoros did her graduate work here at Albrecht University, and she might hire me if she likes my ideas. Working for Rebecca Danforth would be an honor, but the job won't be easy to get. I'm up against engineers from places like MIT and Stanford, the type of people who redesign a mainframe during the week and save a small village during the weekend."

"You save people on weekends, too," she said, her gaze sincere. "You spent most of today helping people who work across the hall from you. Not only that, you donated a huge chunk of time for Annette's experiment."

He'd also signed a petition against programs that weren't inclusive, which included Tia's self-sufficiency seminars. If she thought he wanted to screw-up her internship, she'd have good reason to detest him.

Shit. He didn't want Tia Garcia to hate him. He wanted her to like him.

She stopped munching. "Why aren't you eating?"

"Once I start, I won't stop. Wanted to give you first crack at the popcorn."

"There's plenty for both of us. Go ahead, dig in. A Mountain Man like you needs fuel."

"I can survive on very little." After so many months of loneliness, this simple conversation tasted like a feast. Every word that dropped out of her mouth nourished him in ways nothing else had. "You've seen what I can do to a plate of cookies. I'm not going to dig in until you're full."

"If you think I'm not capable of fighting for a handful of popcorn once you begin eating, you're mistaken." She tossed a kernel at him.

The popcorn bounced off his chin. Felt good to be the target of her attention. "Throwing food at me will only make me like you more."

"I doubt that'll happen. I'm a psychologist, so there's very little chance you'll like me much." She grinned as she said the words, but her mouth contained a sad tilt. "You have good reason to despise anyone in my profession after you were hurt so badly by a therapist."

The past eight months might've turned out differently if his ex had sought help from a different therapist, one who was willing to hear his side of the story. If he'd been able to explain why he'd lost his temper, he might've parted from his ex under much better circumstances, without all the ugly fighting. He might've remained in his original apartment, with his furniture and his clothes. He might've preserved his reputation.

Or not.

Even if he'd gotten out of his dead-end relationship with Stacy, his pain and frustration would've driven him to make different mistakes. He knew that, now.

That anger still had a firm grip on him. His rage had targeted anyone who refused to listen. Therapists and members of The Women's Grid had become his new bull's eye, but he hadn't bothered to speak with anyone in these groups. It was much easier to be pissed off at someone you didn't know.

"Maybe I needed to be misunderstood by that therapist," he admitted. "The experience forced me to take a hard look at myself. To be honest, I didn't like what I saw. Still don't, sometimes. I can be a self-righteous bastard."

"You don't strike me that way. You're strong-willed, but not intolerant. You're hungry, too." Tia pointed to the popcorn. "Eat."

"Not until you're full." His stomach growled, loud and low.

"If you won't feed yourself, I will." She rested one elbow on the armrest and showed him a piece of popcorn. Her mouth curled into a mischievous grin. "Open the barn door and let the cow in."

He laughed and waved her off.

She laughed and dropped the popcorn. "Ack! I lost your snack. Give me more."

Her hand dove into the popcorn, nudging the bucket against Ivan's groin. His sexual fuse caught fire, throwing sparks from his pounding heart to the soles of his feet. Something raw and feral bunched in muscles. Need. Want. Lust. He wanted her to forget about the stupid popcorn and reach into his jeans.

Welcome back, Mr. Caveman.

She held up another kernel, the silver ring around her finger glinting in the theater's dim light. "Open up."

"Fine." He opened his mouth and closed his eyes. A fluffy piece of popcorn landed on his bottom lip and fell onto his tongue. Butter and salt melted into his mouth. He flattened the fluffy piece of corn between his molars with one hard clamp of his jaw.

Soft fingertips grazed his cheek. The caress drifted along his beard, down to the edge of his chin.

Tia was touching him, for no reason, and the gentle way she cupped his jaw calmed him more than a glass of booze ever could.

"I had no idea computer guys were so hot."

He opened his eyes. The theater was dark, the screen bright.

Tia pulled back as though the film's sudden start had surprised her, too.

The camera panned to a woman in a skin-tight dress. She sashayed toward a man hunched over a desktop computer. The fabric of her dress stretched tight across her curvy hips. "So, Hot Computer Guy, what's wrong with my computer?"

"You need a new motherboard, among other things."

"How much is a motherboard?"

"A few hundred bucks."

"I don't have that kind of money." She twirled a blonde curl around her finger, her heavily made-up eyes tapering into a suggestive leer. "Is there another way I can pay for the repair?"

Tia leaned close. "What kind of movie is this?"

"Some D-list flick. This place shows some avant-garde stuff." And he was okay with that, because Tia Garcia's shoulder was pressed against his.

Hot Computer Guy shrugged. "Sorry, ma'am, but a bad motherboard is the least of your problems. You'd better get a new computer, because your benchmark capsule is fried."

"What's a benchmark capsule?" Tia whispered.

"There's no such thing. And no self-respecting IT guy would have a cheap protractor like the one tucked into that actor's shirt pocket." Ivan scowled at the screen.

The actress trailed a long, pink nail down Hot Computer Guy's shirt. "I can't afford a new system, but I can barter for a repair. Maybe I can boot your system while you boot mine."

"Lady, I'm a professional. Do *not* unbutton my pants. Oh, what the hell. My tool could use some handling. Oh yeah, baby. That's right. Grip my joystick."

Tia laughed out loud.

"I've seen enough." Ivan grabbed a giggling Tia by the hand, pulled her out of the theater, and tossed the popcorn into a trash receptacle.

His cell phone vibrated with an unwelcome text.

"Congratulations! You've survived the experiment. Report to Henry's apartment to remove your biofeedback wristband and say goodbye to your partner. You're done!"

Chapter Eight

Ivan rubbed the strip of bare skin on his wrist. The hair that used to grow there was gone, ripped off by that diabolical biofeedback device. Felt like the tight wristband was still there, an invisible reminder of the time he'd spent with Tia.

That time was over. He was back in his apartment. Alone, again. Situation normal. He dragged his eyes back to the experiment's final survey question on his laptop.

Last of all, thank you for participating in the experiment. Summarize your experience in the space below.

Ivan typed one word: STELLAR.

That covered everything. While he was with Tia, he felt an out-of-this-world kind of happy. Not because he was finally with his hot next-door neighbor, but because she was surprisingly upbeat and stunningly kind, more impressive than a line of perfect code and more fun than skating on fresh ice. And even though she ran women-only seminars, she listened to the reasons why he wanted programs like hers to include men.

His point of view seemed to matter to her. If he'd had more time with her, he might've been able to piece together some sort of compromise. Too bad the experiment was over.

Ivan scrolled to the bottom of the survey and pressed send.

What now? He could sleep, but the empty mattress in his bedroom wasn't calling his name. He could eat, but he'd held off on buying groceries to cobble together some money to fix the dent in Tia's car. He could fine-tune his presentation for the Phoros interview, but he couldn't sit still. His body twitched for something more.

Something like Tia.

Thirty minutes had passed since he'd said goodbye to her in Henry's apartment. She might still be awake. He could ask her out on a date.

Bad idea, Einstein. In a few weeks, he'd leave campus. A short time later, Tia would begin her post-doctorate work. If he ended up in Boston and she moved to Denver, they'd never see each other.

A sharp pain pinged behind his eyes. He should probably take out his contacts and go horizontal, but sleep wouldn't ease this restless craving inside him.

"Screw it." He strode out of his apartment, headed for Tia's apartment, and knocked on her door.

Silence.

He knocked again, louder. "Tia? It's Ivan."

"Just a minute."

He pulled a hand through his hair. His fingers snagged on a curl near his ear. Hell, he needed a haircut but he wasn't going to get one until he paid Tia's repair bill. Everything in his life seemed to hinge on her.

It felt like a privilege, not a burden.

"Did you bring a benchmark capsule for me?" she said from somewhere inside her apartment.

He chuckled. "Sorry, Boots. No capsules, here. Are you going to open the door?"

"Nope. I'm not dressed for company. I'm in pajamas."

Visions of black lace draped over tawny breasts danced through his head. "What kind of pajamas?"

"Feels funny talking to you through the door. Maybe we should have this conversation via text."

"I don't like texts. Feels like I'm talking to a machine." He ground a knuckle into the corner of his aching eye. "So what kind of pajamas? Give me details."

"They're comfortable and gray. What's up?"

"I've been thinking about all of the steps we went through on Friday night." He leaned down to peer at the cloudy peephole in case she was there, looking at him. "Step one to a deeper friendship is visual contact, which is something we should strive for. We are neighbors, after all."

Nothing. Not a sound.

He rubbed his sleeve on the peephole but couldn't remove the cloudy film. "I love looking at you. I do it every chance I get. In the gym, in the parking lot, in the lobby."

The quiet thickened.

"The second step is eye-to-eye," he continued, feeling a dark swoop of energy. "Your warm brown eyes on mine. Me trying to figure out what you're thinking."

"I'm thinking that it's odd to hear you recite Desmond Morris's twelve steps to physical intimacy." Her voice sounded closer, clearer. "I didn't think you liked going through those steps."

"I liked being with you. By the way, we've made verbal contact, which is step three. I'm talking to you in a low murmur to soothe your worries. You're talking to me with a brusque edge in your voice, maybe because you're embarrassed I caught you in pajamas." He looked down at his jeans and T-shirt. "I'm in pajamas, too. Sort of."

"Sort of doesn't count. What's the fourth step?"

"Touching hands. You with that silver ring on your finger, mine with the knuckle that didn't heal well." Now that knuckle was swollen and slightly red, which happened whenever he got agitated.

"How did you hurt your knuckle? I've been wondering."

"Someone skated over my hand during a college hockey game. I don't know what hurt worse, the injury or missing the rest of the season." He rubbed his forehead, but the painful throb behind his skull didn't ease. An ibuprofen might help. There was a bottle in his bathroom cabinet, but he didn't want to walk away. "Why do you call me Mountain Man?"

"Because you're big and outdoorsy. What's step five?"

"My arm around your shoulder. Not my favorite step. Feels like I'm back in seventh grade, trying to make a move on Jenny Bannister even though I had a mouthful of braces. All of that hardware was probably the reason I got through middle school hockey with all my teeth."

Tia laughed.

He loved that sound. "By the way, step six involves putting my arm around your waist. Holding you close. My new favorite pastime."

The door opened and Tia peered around the edge. "I'm worried that this experiment manufactured an intimacy between us that isn't real, Ivan. We should probably give ourselves some space."

"I don't want space." He also didn't want to sound like a barking dog, but the ache behind his eyes had gotten worse. He squinted past the pain and attempted a softer tone. "I want to see you again. May I take you to dinner, tomorrow?"

She peeked a little further around the door. Her skin looked damp, like she'd just washed her face. No makeup. Just her, with dark eyes pinned on him and a faint hint of freckles on the rise of her cheekbones.

He rubbed his temple, struggling to focus all of his attention on her. "I want to apologize for taking you to that movie. I didn't know it would be a porno flick."

"That's okay." She tilted her head. "Do you have a headache?"

"Yeah. No big deal." His stomach growled, hungrier than a mosquito on a mannequin.

"Do you get headaches when you're hungry? Maybe you should eat something."

"I already did. The piece of popcorn you fed me was hella-filling." He grinned. The screw of pain tightened behind his eyes.

"You're wincing. That's not good." She tugged him inside and nudged him into a chair at her table. "Pork or chicken? Never mind. I'll give you both."

"Both what? Hey, come back here."

"You need food." She opened the refrigerator and placed a cold beer in front of him.

He handed back the bottle with a matter-of-fact shrug. "I don't drink."

"Okay." She lifted a white carton. "Milk?"

"That's fine." Better than fine. He was inside Tia's apartment and she was dressed in soft-looking gray leggings that clung to her long legs. Her flannel top had the words *on vacation 'til forever* on the front. The fabric hugged her breasts, which moved every time she did. Clearly, she wasn't wearing a bra, and there was nothing more fascinating to him than the sight of Tia Garcia dressed in nothing but comfortable pajamas.

He propped his chin in one hand and watched her reach into a cabinet for a glass. The hem of her shirt lifted, providing a tantalizing glimpse of her sweet round butt encased in gray cotton. "Every time I look at you, the world tilts and my head spins."

"Because you're hungry." She poured him a tall glass of milk. "Drink this while I heat some food in the microwave."

The milk was sweet and creamy. He drained the contents in five long swallows and wiped his mouth on his sleeve like any mountain man would do.

The microwave dinged. Tia set a plate in front of him,

along with a fork. "Be careful, the empanadas are hot."

Steam rose from the meat pies, bathing his face with fragrant spices he couldn't begin to name. As he stared at the unexpected feast in front of him, he wondered what he did to deserve such kindness.

Tia touched the back of his neck. "Go ahead, Ivan. Eat."

His skin tingled from her brief caress and his soul warmed at the worry in her gaze. He cut into the flaky pastry, and savory pork whiffed into his nose. One bite confirmed what he already suspected. This woman cooked as well as his brothers. Feeling closer to home than he'd felt the whole time he'd been in Vermont, he wolfed down both empanadas. At some point while he ate, Tia refilled his glass. He drank every swallow of foamy milk and sighed.

"Want more?"

"No. I'm full." He curled his fingers around her wrist with the same care he'd use if he held a glass bulb. "I had no idea how much I needed food. Thank you, Tee."

"You're welcome."

"This is the third time you fed me. I owe you."

She shook her head. "I'm not keeping score."

"I am. First, you gave me cookies. Then popcorn. And now empanadas." He rose to his feet and stepped close. She smelled of bedtime rituals that included toothpaste and soap. Simple yet intimate things he hadn't expected to discover when he'd pounded on her door.

She pulled her wrist out of his hand, grabbed a sponge, and wiped off the counter even though the kitchen was spotless.

"I'm beginning to see a pattern," he told her. "You move away when you're uncomfortable. You did it when we sat on your couch last night, probably because you were nervous. You did it in Lotza Pizza when you saw that woman. You just did it now, and I'd like to know why. What's wrong?"

"My stomach is tied in a knot and I can't take a deep breath." She tossed the sponge into the sink and turned toward him. "I didn't expect you to show up, tonight. The things you said surprised me. You always catch me off guard. Whenever I expect you to do one thing, you do the opposite. I want to read you right, but I can never figure out what you're thinking."

"If I were thinking, I would've stayed in my apartment rather than bang on your door late at night. Around you, all I do is react. My pulse screams in the shell of my ears and my mind spins like a hard drive with a seized spindle. You know what's weird? I like the feeling." And that wasn't all, not by a long shot. "I like *you*."

Her brown eyes opened wide. She pressed her teeth into her bottom lip as if she didn't know what to say.

Not exactly the reaction he'd hoped for. He hid his uneasiness behind a brusque nod and carried his dish to the sink. "Where do you keep the dish soap?"

"Under the sink."

"So do I. Don't like seeing bottles on the counter." He opened the cabinet. Sure enough, there was a neat row of cleaning products within easy reach. He squirted some dishwashing soap onto the plate and made short work of cleaning the smear of sauce from the plain white china. "Dishtowel?"

"Here." She handed him a blue one.

He smirked. "Do you own anything that isn't blue?"

"I have a yellow duck."

"True." He'd brought her that bright little duck. It was still on the coffee table in her living room, which was a good sign. And now Ivan was in this cheerful kitchen, drying a plate after a much-needed meal. The twitchy feeling inside him eased. His head no longer pounded. Best of all, Tia stood beside him.

For how long? Any day now, the ghost of his mistake would materialize. Tia would learn that he'd left his ex-girlfriend when she needed him most of all, that he was capable of losing his temper in the worst possible way, that a six-pack of beer could turn him into a screaming monster.

Hating those memories, he put away the clean plate. It was past midnight. He should probably go, but he took some extra time to hang the dishtowel over the oven handle. A stall tactic, but he couldn't stop himself. Every neuron in his body wanted to stay, because he'd finally found someone who wanted to read him right.

Tia looked up at him. "Are you feeling better?"

"Much." The word splintered in his throat. She was a mind-blowing combination of stunning beauty and pure kindness, wrapped in touchable soft gray fleece. He ached to explore her pretty curves, but he'd been invited into her home for food, nothing else. This was not the right time to act on this primitive need inside him, but he couldn't stop looking at her. Couldn't stop wanting her.

Pink rose on the ridge of Tia's cheekbones. "There's a crumb on your whiskers."

Oh, great. He wiped a hand across the lower half of his face and bumped into the oven. The dishtowel fell off the handle and landed on the floor. He bent to pick up the towel and rammed his shoulder into the edge of the counter like a too-big grizzly bear in a too-small cage. He slapped the towel over the oven handle and straightened, breathing as though he'd just bench-pressed three hundred pounds.

"The crumb is still there." She lifted her hand until those fingertips stopped a few inches from his face. "Can I?"

"Yeah, fine." He stayed still and tried not to look like he was dying to jump on her.

She touched a spot near the corner of his mouth. The gentle pressure of her fingers eased and then returned. "You've got some blond whiskers near your bottom lip, mixed in with all the brown ones."

Being the object of her curiosity was better than being the cause of her wariness, so he let her explore. He gazed into her eyes, close enough to see the tiny slivers of gold in her irises. Close enough to taste the sweet spearmint on her breath. Close enough to study that fine line where downy skin met her smooth lips. That pink skin made him think of other parts that might be the same color, the same slick texture. He wanted all of those private pink parts, but he didn't move a muscle. He'd let her get used to him. If he took his time, he might persuade her to feel safe whenever he was around.

Her hand drifted along his jaw and moved down his neck, a light caress along the sensitive skin of his throat. And then she smiled. A slow, soft one she'd never given him before. One that glimmered in her eyes as though she liked touching his rough edges.

Something fierce jolted through him. He lurched forward and kissed her lips, hard. Too hard. This contained none of the tenderness that pounded in his chest, no. This was an I wanna fuck your mouth with my tongue, give it to me or I'll die type of kiss, messy and crass and out of control, accompanied by a thick grunt and all ten fingers shoved into her hair, hauling her closer, trapping her between his damp palms and thundering heart.

"God, Tia. *This.*" This was so good, it hurt. This was dirty and raw and the best thing he'd ever done. He claimed her mouth again, not able to get enough of that lush softness. Good lord, this woman was made to be kissed. Her lips were the softest, silkiest things on earth, and his. All his, now. He couldn't stop this feverish plundering, this impatient need. His breath came and went in harsh, raspy grunts. Every tendon inside him stretched close to bursting. His pulse banged in the back of his eyes and the base of his balls.

She felt better than anything he'd ever touched. Soft and silky and strong and female in a way that was pure Tia, who gave more than she ever took. All of this giving was something he needed more than he needed food. This went far beyond want or desire. Those things paled to this lunatic need inside him.

Lunatic? *Shit.*

He froze, panting against her lips. Lips that were swollen, hot. Had he hurt her? God, no. He didn't want to hurt her. Ever. Gently, he pulled his hands out of her hair. He inched back to give her room to breathe, to move.

To give her a choice.

"I should've asked before I touched you," he admitted, hating that he'd gone caveman on her. "This is what I want. To be close to you. To kiss you. Is that okay?"

"More than okay." She twined her arms around the back of his neck and pressed a brief, happy nibble against his mouth. And then another on his bottom lip, her eyes glimmering with something that looked a helluva lot like desire.

She wanted this.

She wanted him.

A hard thrust of joy thrummed through him. He traced her mouth with his, starting at the fullness of her bottom lip and working his way, millimeter by millimeter, to one corner of her mouth and then the other, mapping the landscape of her stellar lips into his brain. This was one roadmap he wanted to learn fast and travel often.

Her lips parted. The tip of her tongue touched his.

The invitation almost dropped him to his knees. He deepened the kiss and hauled her close, losing his mind when her breasts squished against his chest. He was her Mountain Man now, powered by lust and acting on instinct, no longer a robot trapped in a computer lab. "You, in my arms. Me, lit up by your kiss. Us, the one word I've been dying to say."

She smiled. "Us?"

"Yeah. You and me. Us." The word came out firm. Certain. The caveman inside him wanted to grab two handfuls of her ass, but he spread his hands along her lower back and kept his touch gentle. Reassuring. "You and me. For dinner. Us, on a date. I want to convince you to get all up in my business. Does tomorrow night work for you?"

"I wish it did, but I offered to lead Annette's anxiety management support group tomorrow night."

"Fine. What about Monday?"

"Sounds good."

"It's a date, then." He sealed the deal with a kiss, slow and soft and hard and hot until they were both out of breath.

"Okay, wow. Um, we'd better stop." Tia let go of him and tucked a hair behind her ear. "It's late. We should probably say goodnight."

"Hm? Oh, right." He stepped back, his dick a steel pole and his brain a lump of mush. "Goodnight, then."

"'Night." She gave him a brief kiss on his cheek. And then another one on his jaw. And another one that slid toward the corner of his mouth. She sighed and nuzzled his bottom lip. "There's time for one more kiss. Maybe two more."

"You can have as many as you want." Because he had an infinite loop of kisses for Tia Garcia.

"No, wait. I should stop. This goodnight but kiss me more time thing isn't very fair to either of us." She eased away, her dark eyes lusty and apologetic at the same time.

"Sorry for the mixed messages."

"You never have to apologize for getting me amped up. I relish the feeling. Turn me on every night. Mornings, too. Hell, meet me for lunch and drive me crazy. No complaints, here. Just give me a second to cool off before I walk out of here." He tugged at the denim that stretched across his throbbing dick.

Her gaze zipped down to the fly of his jeans and back up. "Cooling off is a smart idea. We should think of something completely asexual, like tiny ducks in teacups."

"Ducks in teacups remind me of you." He shoved both hands into his pockets so he wouldn't reach for her again. "I'll think about number theory."

"Good. I'll focus on cognitive neuroscience." She looked up at the ceiling, contemplating. "Some deep thought about neural connections might numb my swollen parts."

Aw, hell. This topic wouldn't deflate his dick, but he asked anyway. "Which parts? Be specific."

"Shh. I'm thinking about my amygdala."

"Is yours swollen?" He was pretty sure his was.

"No. The amygdala is a set of neurons in the brain that processes emotions. If you could peer deep into my medial temporal lobe, you'd see that my amygdala is round, slick, and glossy."

"Fascinating." His brain buffered into thoughts of other things that were round, slick, and glossy. He leaned close enough to breathe in the clean, sweet scent of her. "I want to know more."

"Nope, this isn't working. My cerebral cortex can't

stop thinking about kissing you." She walked toward the door. "Time to go, Mountain Man. Head home so I can take care of myself."

"Fine. I'm going." He took three steps and put on the brakes. "What do you mean by *take care of* yourself?"

Her tawny cheeks turned bubble-gum pink. She fiddled with the hem of her shirt and shrugged. "You know what I mean."

"No, I don't. I haven't the foggiest." But he had his suspicions. The smooth skin at the base of her throat contained a dark, red flush of excitement and she was breathing fast. Her nipples poked against her soft shirt as though they needed to be sucked. Her sexual agitation felt like a hot prickle against his electrified skin. How would she expend all of that heat? "Please don't say you're going to do yoga or meditate."

"Heck, no. I'm going to touch myself."

Oh. Hell. Yes. "Let me help."

"I don't need help. A self-sufficient woman can take care of herself."

"Can I watch?"

"No!" She smothered a laugh and poked him in the side. "I don't need an audience."

"Don't write off an audience until you consider all of the benefits." He raised his eyebrows in an attempt to look earnest. "I could hold something for you, Tee."

"Like an iced tea?"

"I was thinking more along the lines of a breast or a thigh." Or that stellar booty.

"No, thanks. All I need is my favorite toy."

"Toy?" His voice cracked like brittle wire. "What toy?"

"It's six inches long, bright blue, and vibrates." Smiling like she couldn't wait to rub one out, she opened the door. "Bye."

He stopped on the threshold, all two hundred and thirty aroused pounds of him dying to know more. "What will you think about when you 'take care of' yourself?"

"Well, since you asked." Her kiss-moistened lips curled into a slow smile. "I'll be thinking about the hungry way you look at me whenever you call me Tee."

A firm push propelled him into the hallway. He pivoted on one heel in time to see the door close.

"*Tia*. Gah!" He leaned down a few inches to stare at the peephole, but couldn't see a thing. Every atom in his body knew she stood near the other side of the door, waiting for him to leave.

What kind of idiot would ever leave her?

Him, that's who. As soon as he finished his degree, he'd pack up his laptop, throw his meager possessions into the back of Sturdy Stella, and start his real life. The one where he earned gobs of money and buried his imperfect past under a successful career in computer technology. Once he moved to Boston, there would be no dread that someone would recognize his name for all the wrong reasons.

He glanced toward his apartment. The building supervisor had finally changed the flickering bulb in the ceiling fixture. Gray-green fluorescent light bathed the hall in various shades of blah, which seemed appropriate. His life was blah until Tia rebooted his system. He was damn sure his biofeedback levels would tank the instant he walked away from her.

Yeah, it sucked that he was about to move to Boston and she'd eventually head to Denver, but he'd think of a way to make this work. He could solve any problem, right? All he had to do was convince her to give him a chance.

But that might not happen if she heard he was an alcoholic with an anger problem.

CHAPTER NINE

Getting rid of a large, aroused computer engineer wasn't easy. Tia wanted to drag him into her bedroom, but mindless lust could lead to regret. She'd felt that regret ever since she dated a good-looking doctor who happened to have a wife and daughter. To prevent another mistake, she'd take things slow with Ivan until she knew more about him.

She'd find out more tonight, during their dinner date. Ivan was surprisingly open about who he was, what he wanted, and how he felt. Would he be willing to open up even more? She longed to why he'd sought help from a therapist who'd refused to hear his side of the story, but she didn't feel right about asking. Why should Ivan trust her to safeguard his answer if she wasn't willing to trust him to do something quite straightforward, like fix her car?

He'd been asking for her trust, in various ways, for a

long time. He'd cleared the snow off her windshield for months, tried to speak to her every time they met, and definitely wanted to demonstrate that he was a good man. Putting her faith in someone was difficult, but she could let him take care of that small dent in her car. There was no guarantee he'd fix the problem the same way she would, but he'd asked for the chance to make things right. Repeatedly.

If she trusted him, she might convince him to trust her.

She grabbed her phone and texted Ivan.

Boots: Could I take you up on your offer to fix my car?
Mountain Man: You bet. I found a guy who does mobile repairs. He might be able to take care of dent, today. I'll make an appointment and let you know.
Boots: Ok. Thx.

Well, that was fast. And easy. Sounded like Ivan had begun to solve her problem long before she'd asked for help. Warmed by a sudden wave of relief, Tia gathered her things and left her apartment.

The Monday morning sky was cluttered with clouds. A frigid wind stole her breath like a too-tight belt. She unlocked her car in case the mobile mechanic needed to open her door, made sure there was nothing valuable inside, and walked toward campus hunched inside her coat. The Counseling Center's warm, tranquil atmosphere felt great after schlepping across campus.

She checked to see what appointments she had for

the day and then walked into the conference room for the weekly staff meeting. When she settled into a chair at the table, everything seemed normal among the interns. Annette asked if she was going to the four o'clock yoga class. Kristin texted and talked at the same time, as usual. And Wayne glared at the screen of his digital tablet as if the intensity of his stare would change the growth forecast for his stock portfolio.

Annette and Kristin veered off on a discussion about Henry, the guy who'd helped them design the biofeedback devices for their experiment. Tia listened half-heartedly as she added a few tasks to her to-do list.

Buy milk. Check the post-doctoral listserv for updates on the Denver job. Sign up for conference in NYC.

"Mind telling me what happened on Saturday night?"

Tia looked up, surprised to see Wayne's gaze pointed at her. "Beg pardon?"

"You were with your neighbor, the one who dinged your car."

"We had to spend a few hours together for the experiment."

"I know, but you were holding his arm." Wayne shifted in his seat. His mouth sloped down like a steep ski trail. "Looked like you two were a thing."

"Wait. What?" Annette swiveled toward Tia. "Did something happen between you and Ivan?"

"Um…" The fact that she'd kissed him as though his mouth was more essential than air kinda meant something happened, but that something felt too poignant to gossip about.

Wayne braced a hand on the back of Tia's chair, his arm stiff and straight. "Are you dating him, or not? Because if you're dating him, I don't get it. He looks like a rabid grizzly bear."

"Well, this is interesting." Kristin smirked. "Are you jealous, Wayne?"

He yanked his hand off the back of Tia's chair. "No, not jealous. I'm concerned. He's one of those moronic windbags who complained about Tia's seminars, for one thing. He doesn't support you. He doesn't understand what you're trying to do. Why get anywhere near that jerk?"

Because he tastes like almonds didn't seem like a very good answer.

Dr. Solomon entered the room and settled into the spot at the head of the table. "I'm sorry I'm late. Before we get started, did any of you hear about what happened this weekend? Apparently, someone planted signs in the residential quad."

Tia was the only one who nodded. "I saw those signs on Saturday night. There were five posters, all written in the same handwriting, with messages like *bust walls, not balls* and *if toxic masculinity is a thing, so is poisonous femininity.*"

"Those signs must've been planted by the people who are pushing for every program to be inclusive, and I can see their point." Dr. Solomon opened a copy of the campus newspaper. "Look at this headline. More than fifteen hundred people have signed a petition against any club or group that discriminates against men. The push and pull between the men and women on campus is intensifying. People are talking about this. It's spilled into social media."

"Because of that hairy goon," Wayne muttered to Tia. "Look at what he's done."

"All he's done is ask to attend some seminars," Tia hissed back.

"I've talked to the administration," Dr. Solomon continued. "The University understands that in order to treat specific problems, a small portion of our programming must be targeted to women. Same goes for the programs we offer for men. However, we have a small problem." Dr. Solomon closed the newspaper and looked at Tia. "I'm afraid the CEO of Blisspea Enterprises decided she doesn't want to speak at your Entrepreneurs in Technology seminar. She called me ten minutes ago and said she's concerned that if she participates, someone will accuse her, or her company, of being anti-male."

Tia's heart tripped. "But I invited her to speak about entrepreneurship. How is that topic anti-male?"

"Because she'd be appearing on behalf of your SelfWell seminar series, which serves the women on campus. Anything that excludes men is under fire, no matter how well-intentioned." Dr. Solomon's expression firmed. "We're going to have to tweak your program, Tia. You too, Wayne. Make sure to offer some of your seminars to everyone."

Wayne slouched in his chair. "I doubt any woman will

be interested in How to Win at Fantasy Football and Life."

"Don't allow your prejudices to influence your interactions." Dr. Solomon's sharp gaze moved around the room, landing on every counselor and intern. "The services offered by the Counseling Center must be available to everyone on campus. We need to be able to serve all populations, not just a few groups. If someone needs your help, you'll provide support."

Tia's worries rose like fat in day-old stew. "Many of my seminars won't work well with a mixed audience. The seminar on female sexuality, in particular. If men attend, I think some women will have great difficulty admitting they don't know how to climax."

"I agree. Sexuality seminars are some of the programs that tend to work best in small, controlled groups. That being said, you might be surprised by how compassionate men can be about any problem that affects women."

Well, that was a stab in the heart. How could she possibly know how compassionate men could be when her own father took off when she was eight? She was right in the middle of showing him the macaroni necklace she'd made when he turned on his heel, grabbed a tin of chewing tobacco, and walked out. Granted, the macaroni necklace wasn't her finest work, but still.

Tia's nose stung. She sniffled and reached for a tissue.

Annette leaned toward her. "Are you crying?"

"No, but my nose runs when I'm upset." She pressed the tissue against her left nostril, which had started to drip. "I don't know if I'm a good candidate to counsel men, Dr. Solomon. I've always wanted to help women be strong and independent, so all of my graduate work is focused on women. My thesis is on women. I *know* women. To be honest, there are times when I can't read men."

"Your insecurities are also your strengths," said Dr. Solomon in a gentle voice. "You can relate to other people's insecurities. The key is to not let your fears impede your growth as a psychologist."

"You're right." Tia wiped her nose. "But if I can't trust my instincts about what someone is trying to say, how can I help them?"

"If you're feeling lost, you can always ask someone to clarify how they're feeling." Dr. Solomon folded her hands, serene yet insistent. "You have two seminars left in your SelfWell series. Can you open them to men?"

"I can't. Every seat is taken. All of my small group sessions are fully booked too, including the one this afternoon."

"Perhaps you can book a larger room for your seminars," Dr. Solomon suggested. "I know there's not a lot of time to adapt your program to include men, but see what you can do."

Inviting men into one of her group sessions could backfire. Women might not participate or even attend. Could she risk that? Would she miss the chance to help someone if she kept men out of the discussion? If men showed up, would a stone-faced guy complain if she didn't read him right?

Tia crushed the tissue in her hand and shoved those concerns aside. There was only one question she needed

CHAPTER TEN

A few hours later, Ivan closed the small gray door on the robot's back. The last time he attempted to do this, white stuffing ended up all over the floor and an eye flew across the room. That carnage might happen again, but he needed to prove his photovoltaic battery had enough juice to run a high-tech instrument. It probably wasn't a good idea to reprogram the robot on so little rest, but he needed to film this video for his upcoming interview with Phoros Technologies.

He pointed his phone at the robot, turned on the video app, and tucked a small stuffed animal into the curve of the robot's metal arm. "Omega, pet the dog."

The robot woke with a soft whir. One metal hand curled around the toy's body, determining the size and weight of the object. Laser beam eyes mapped the surface of the toy. With slow, steady movements, a steel hand eased down the toy's back in a gentle stroke.

"Nice work, Omega. Keep going." Ivan recorded for thirty seconds and downloaded the video to his laptop.

Henry strolled into the lab and halted by the robot. "Why is Omega purring?"

"He's whirring, not purring. I put a new battery into his heart. He seems to like it." Ivan opened his web browser, navigated to the Phoros Technologies website, and clicked on the tab for employment. Another research and development job had been added, with a starting salary close to ninety thousand dollars. If he made that kind of money, he'd never have to eat another peanut butter sandwich on stale bread. He could afford a decent place to live, with decent furniture. He could keep Sturdy Stella safe in his garage and buy a new car that didn't stall.

With a new set of wheels, he could visit Tia while she finished her internship here in Vermont. The drive from Boston would be close to three hours, one way. It was a long trip, but worth the mileage if he could see her on weekends.

"This new battery of yours is fantastic." Henry bent close to the robot. "I've never seen Omega move so smoothly."

"I added some lines to his code and sent you a copy of the file."

"You're the bomb dot com." On his way to his desk, Henry glanced at Ivan's computer screen. "If you keep staring at the Phoros website, you'll have every word memorized."

"I'm trying to read between the lines so I can give them good reason to hire me."

"Tell them the truth. You've got three patents and a genius IQ."

"I'd rather be wanted for more than my brain." Story of his life.

"Then tell them you never stop working. That'll get their attention." Henry sat at his desk and opened a brown paper bag from Hungry Hank's.

The rich scent of deli meat and Italian seasoning filled the room. Ivan's stomach howled like a dog on a chain.

"Sounds like you swallowed a beagle." Henry offered half of a hoagie. "Want some?"

"No thanks, Stretch. I packed a sandwich." A boring peanut butter one. Rather than reach for it, Ivan opened a new browser window and signed into his bank account. Good, his paycheck had been deposited an hour ago. There was more than enough money to cover a night out with Tia.

Eric Stanwick sauntered into the room with a smirk on his face and a cast on his arm. "I just heard that one of the interns from the Campus Counseling Center is offering a group session today. No men allowed, of course. A bunch of us are going to show up."

Ivan frowned. "And do what?"

"Give them grief for not including men."

"Bad idea. Storming into a seminar is a rotten way to convince anyone to include us."

Stanwick rolled his eyes. "If we do nothing, nothing will change."

"Change won't happen if we act like a bunch of spiteful Neanderthals."

"They already think we're a bunch of Neanderthals. I'm not gonna stand by while this toxic masculinity myth gains strength. I think we need to do something, now." Eric lifted his phone. "Take a look at my social media feed. Everyone agrees with me."

"I don't. If we stoop to bullying, we're just as bad as The Women's Grid." Ivan leaned back in his chair, willing to include Stanwick in the quest to shut down The Grid. "Tag along with me when I speak to the Dean of Students on Thursday."

"Talking isn't working, Antonov. Actions speak louder than words. I'm taking a stand." Stanwick stalked into the hallway and bellowed, "Rise up, men. Bust walls, not balls!"

Henry shook his head. "Why doesn't he get this fired up about work?"

"Because he's all about the retweets." Ivan opened up a new browser window to find the university's website. Didn't take long to find the Counseling Center's page. *Join us at one o'clock in room 209 of the Student Center to talk about finding the courage to open up to friends, to loved ones, to people who disagree with you. Our intern, Tia Garcia, will help you find ways to tap into the courage to be true to yourself in a way that's kind to others. This is part of the SelfWell program focused on women. UPDATE: This seminar is full. All twenty-five seats are taken. Contact the Counseling Center if you'd like to learn about our programs.*

"Shit. Those dopes are going to disrupt Tia's seminar." Ivan shoved away from the desk and stood. "I've gotta get to her before they do."

Henry stopped chewing a mouthful of hoagie, unaware of the piece of lettuce stuck to his chin. "Want me to come with you?"

"No. Stay here and find out what's going on. Text me if you learn anything." Ivan jogged out of the room, dodged students on his way down the stairwell, and burst out of Harris Hall.

He sprinted toward the center of campus. A nasty wind bit through the thin fabric of his shirt and ice pellets pelted his face, but he didn't give a damn. All he wanted to do was make sure Tia was safe, and then find the misguided clods who thought it would be a good idea to bother her.

When he arrived at the Student Center, his cell phone dinged with a text from Henry. *Stanwick is on his way with most of the computer engineers from the Robotics group.*

Well, that sucked. Why were those guys following a bozo like Stanwick? Ivan hurried to the information desk, where a bored-looking student sat, stuffing glossy pamphlets into dull envelopes.

Ivan greeted her with a nod. "I need a room that can seat twenty-five people. I know I'm asking at the last minute, but is there anything available right now?"

The girl checked her computer screen. "Room 312 is open until three o'clock."

"That'll work. Sign me up." He slapped his ID on the desk.

She looked at his card, chewed on her thumbnail,

and looked up to take a longer peek at him. "You're Ivan Antinoove?"

"No. The name is Antonov." He stressed the first syllable and rounded out the o's the same way his Slavic relatives would pronounce the word. His pulse kicked up a notch, not because he was annoyed at the mispronunciation of his name, but because of the suspicion he spotted in her gaze. "Is there a problem?"

"Nah. I thought you were someone else. Someone not so nice." She smiled. "Phew, right?"

The hairs on the back of his neck stood straight up. This girl had heard of him, but whoever had thrown his name under the bus had fouled up the pronunciation, which made him relieved and soul-sick at the same time, but he didn't give a ripe fuck what anyone thought of him at the moment, as long as he could get Tia out of danger. "Could I have my card back?"

"Sure. Here ya go." The girl handed over his ID and broke into an I'm-sorry-I-thought-you-were-a-brute smile. "Be sure to turn off the lights when you're—"

He took off, unwilling to hear a desultory lecture about what to do after he was done with the room. Nothing mattered but Tia, so he trotted past the long line of grumpy students near the cafeteria and made his way up to the second floor. Didn't take long to find room 209. He knocked twice and opened the door. Conversation dropped to a dead hush. Twenty-five women turned to look at him.

Tia did, too. She was seated in a chair with her legs crossed, wearing black boots that went up to the hem of her dark skirt. Her hair was loose and long, her blouse crisp and white, her gaze confused but warm.

That warmth made his heart skid like a dull skate on thin ice.

Her eyebrows rose. "Ivan?"

Don't frighten her. He moved toward her and spoke in a low, even tone. "Some men are heading over here."

She blinked. "How many?"

"Seven, maybe more."

"Seven?" She fiddled with her ring and looked around the room. "I think we can make room for more. Will they mind sitting on the floor?"

"Huh?" Oh, hell. She thought Stanwick and his merry band of numbskulls wanted to take part in her seminar. God, if that were only the case. "Listen, they want to crash your seminar in some misguided attempt to make a statement about not being included."

"Oh. I see." She stopped playing with her ring.

"There's an empty room on the third floor. I reserved it for the next two hours. Please, honey, move upstairs now. I don't want anyone to harass you or your group. Come with me." He reached for her hand to help her up, hating that his old hockey injury prevented his index finger from fully closing around her slim palm.

"Let's take a short break and move upstairs to finish our discussion," Tia said to the group as she reached for her purse.

The women followed her lead and filed out of the door. For some reason, everyone headed to the elevator rather than the stairs. Luckily, the lift arrived right away.

Ivan got in last and pressed the button for the third floor.

He didn't have to look to know where Tia was. He could smell the sweet scent of cinnamon cookies to his right.

She touched his sleeve. The brief stroke was nowhere near his skin but he felt the caress all the way to the back of his throat.

"You're covered in sleet," she murmured.

"I didn't have time to grab my coat." He tried to keep the lusty caveman out of his eyes when he glanced at her. The need to grab her gathered deep inside, but he resisted. She was working right now. Not a good time to haul her close for a vigorous kiss, so he settled for a quiet murmur close to her ear. "Your car is fixed. No more dent."

Surprise lit her up like a halogen bulb. "Really?"

"Yeah. I brought the mechanic to your car and he was able to do the repair in the parking lot. Didn't take long. Your car looks brand new." Kind of how he felt. Brand new. Alive again, with a heart that pounded in his chest whenever this woman was near.

"Thank you." She squeezed his forearm.

A blonde peered around Tia's shoulder at him. "Are you a psychologist, too?"

"No. I'm a computer engineer."

"Oh. Still, though, you speak guy language. You might be able to help. We've been talking about my boyfriend, and I'm tired of guessing what he's thinking. He said he'd see me last night, but he stumbled into my room at midnight, drunk as a skunk. What gives? Is he into me, or not?"

A redhead shook her head. "If he showed up drunk, he doesn't respect you, Natalie."

Natalie sighed. "It's not that simple. He had to party at his fraternity or else he'd get grief for leaving early to see me."

Another girl nodded. "Your man can't look like a wimp in front of his frat brothers. Cut him some slack."

The elevator doors opened. Ivan stepped out, glad to escape that conversation, and led the way to the room he reserved.

"Natalie, you skipped our sorority meeting to see him and he showed up four hours late. If you don't have any respect for what's important to you, neither will he."

The redhead had a good point, but Ivan kept his mouth shut. He turned on the lights and surveyed the room. Looked like there were enough chairs for everyone. As the group settled in, he touched Tia's back to assure himself that she was okay.

She looked up at him and smiled.

He kept his hand against her for one more moment. Touching her erased the sick feeling in his gut. With her, he felt good again. "I'll wait downstairs. If anyone shows up, I'll send them away."

Natalie reappeared, arms crossed and one foot tapping on the floor. "You never did answer my question. Do you think my boyfriend is into me, or not?"

"Sounds like he's into his fraternity more than anything else," Ivan admitted. "When a guy is crazy about a woman, he shows up on time. He keeps his promises. And if he thinks she might need him, he busts his ass to find her."

Natalie nodded. "Like you did right now, for Tia."

"Yeah. Like that." He clenched his jaw and walked out, chased by guilt. He wasn't some perfect example of a boyfriend. Far from it. Not long ago, he'd been stuck in a pointless relationship and waited too long to tell his ex how unhappy he was. He'd blindsided her when he couldn't take another day of her wild mood swings. He'd broken up with her when she needed him the most. When her friends in The Women's Grid heard about how he'd handled things, they called him heartless.

They were right.

He hadn't changed. In a few days, he'd meet with the Dean of Students and ask him to defund any program that didn't include men, which would put Tia's program in jeopardy.

What could be more heartless than that?

Chapter Eleven

Three hours after Tia wrapped up her seminar, she could still feel the phantom touch of Ivan's warm hand.

He'd gripped her as though he never wanted to let go. He'd called her honey. And for the first time, his blue eyes contained enough alarm to spill into his expression. She could read him. He was worried. So worried, he hadn't stopped to grab a coat in his rush to find her. The only thing that seemed to matter to Ivan was getting her, and everyone else in the group, into a different room so they wouldn't be hassled by a bunch of angry men.

After the sudden room change, the group session went off without a hitch. Now that Tia finally had a few minutes to herself, she pulled out her phone. When she unlocked the screen, Ivan's number popped up. He'd called an hour ago while she was in a counseling session but didn't leave a message, which made sense. Texting and voicemail weren't his go-to means of communication.

Ivan Antonov preferred to interact in person, which was one of the things that made him so unique.

She didn't have much time before her next appointment showed up, so she sent a brief text.

Boots: Sorry I missed your call. Are we still on for dinner?

MountainMan: Definitely. Does 6:30 work for you?

Boots: Perfect.

MountainMan: BTW, how did your seminar go?

Boots: Very well. Thx for finding a room for us. We weren't interrupted.

MountainMan: I hung out to see if any guys showed up. Seven did.

Boots: Did you speak to them?

MountainMan: Yeah. They won't bother you, again.

Amazing. Even though he had a problem with women-only discussions, he'd sprinted across campus to protect hers.

"Tia?" The Counseling Center's secretary poked her head around the doorway. "Your next appointment is here. Shall I send her in?"

"Yes, thank you." Tia sent one last text to Ivan.

Boots: My client just arrived. Gotta go.

She tucked away her phone and welcomed Pamela into the room. "How are you?"

"Oh, I don't know." Pamela sat across from Tia and fussed with the stack of bracelets on her arm. "I'm worried about Greg."

"Your boyfriend? What's wrong?"

"He's following me around as though he doesn't want

me going anywhere without him. He's, like, afraid I'm going to break up or something. I keep telling him I love him, but he—" She stopped talking and bit her bottom lip.

"You can tell me, Pamela."

"He wants to have sex, like, all the time. The thing is, I've got to study. I feel really guilty when I say no to him."

"Why?" Tia studied Pamela's face. A smooth layer of foundation covered any remnant of the bruise beneath her eyes. "How does he react when you say no to him?"

"Well, he looks sad. Sometimes he mopes. Yesterday, he got a little mad."

Bingo. "When he gets mad, what happens?"

"He won't look at me and he has trouble telling me what's wrong." Pamela fidgeted with her bracelets again. "I know what's bothering him. He's super stressed about getting into law school, but he doesn't want to admit it. His LSAT scores aren't as high as he'd hoped for, but he didn't have much time to prepare for the exam while he was playing football. Being with me helps him feel better. I should support him, not push him away."

Really? Was this man so unstable that he couldn't handle a little stress? Tia's temper cracked. "Pamela, you shouldn't have to tiptoe around Greg. If you need to study, you deserve the freedom to do so. You don't have to be with him all the time. Are you afraid of how he'll react if you disappoint him?"

Pamela's mouth puckered. "What do you mean?"

"Will he hit you?"

"No! Why do you think he would?"

"A short while ago, there was a bruise under your eye."

"That wasn't a bruise. That was a dark circle. I had a sinus infection." She crossed her arms and her legs. "Don't you believe me?"

Of course not. Sinus infections didn't leave marks like that. After witnessing the terrible things men did to the women they supposedly loved, Tia knew a player like Greg would hurt Pamela. That's what guys like him did. They threw punches to get their way. They thought sucking down beers with fraternity brothers was more important than keeping a promise to their girlfriend. If they hooked up with someone for too long, they'd grow bored of the same old, same old. They'd hide their wedding rings in deep pockets and cheat on their wives. When these men found someone else to boink, they'd disappear like dew, never to be seen again.

Tia leaned forward, struggling to keep her voice even. "You said he punched someone at a party. I'm worried he's hitting you, too."

"No, he'd never do that. Never! He hates violence."

"Yet that didn't stop him from starting a brawl."

"That wasn't him, that was the steroids he was taking. He was juicing up, trying to add bulk in the gym, and everything about him changed. He was mad all the time. He wasn't Greg, anymore. I didn't like who he'd become, so I broke up with him. He stopped using right after that."

Really? "How can you be sure he's not using?"

"He's lost the weight he gained with the steroids. He's back to himself. I know he's not lying to me, but that doesn't mean shit, does it?" Pamela shoved herself to the edge of her chair and glared. "You don't believe anything I say. You see a dark circle under my eye and you think I've been hit. You think I'm so desperate for love, I'll stay with a man who mistreats me. That's so wrong. Everything you think about me and Greg is wrong. You don't know him. I do. And now I know you."

"Listen, Pamela, I have to ask these tough questions because I want to protect you."

"From what? From being happy with Greg? It feels like you're trying to stop me from being with him, and I don't know why. I love him and he loves me, but you don't believe that. You only believe what you want to believe, and you think he wants to hurt me. I thought you were my friend, but friends believe each other. You don't. You don't believe he loves me. You think I'm an idiot for loving Greg. I never want to see you again." Pamela burst into tears and raced out of the room as if she was running from the biggest bitch on campus.

Tia stared at the empty chair across from her, stunned. She shot to her feet and jogged into the Counseling Center's lobby, but no Pamela. The blonde was faster than Usain Bolt.

The secretary nodded toward the exit. "She went that way."

Tia opened the door. Snow whipped into her face, making it impossible to see more than a few feet down the sidewalk. This was no gentle spring storm. This was a full-blown blizzard, but the vicious lash of wind hadn't stopped Pamela from running straight into its wrath.

You're trying to stop me from being with him, and I

don't know why.

The answer was easy. This blow up with Pamela was all her fault. Her prejudices about men had poisoned her judgment. She'd never ease someone else's troubles if she couldn't look past her own pain. That pain was always with her, a low-pitched static in the background of her mind. That static had interfered for so long, she couldn't hear anything but that noise.

Embarrassed by the mistakes she'd made, Tia gathered her things and began the long walk back to her apartment. The wicked storm made the trip feel twice as long. Hard arrows of sleet landed on her nose, her cheeks, her lips. The biting wind shoved her hair across her eyes. Snow squirmed into the neckline of her coat and turned her mittens into frozen yarn.

By the time she began to climb the steps to the second floor of her apartment building, she was numb except for the heavy ache of remorse in her chest. All she wanted to do was flop into bed and cry.

If only she could cry like a normal person.

"There's good ice fishing on the lake near Killington." A man's voice drifted down the staircase. The words contained a heavy snap of impatience. "Ruck up some gear and head north with me."

"I can't. I have to work."

That was Ivan's voice, deep and husky. Sounded like he was talking to someone in the hallway. Tia stopped and gazed down at the large, snowy splotches on her coat. She looked like a sick polar bear. She tried to fluff her icy hair, realized there was nothing she could do to look any better, and stepped into the hallway.

Ivan stood in front of his apartment, speaking to a man who towered over him by at least six inches. The stranger had long, dark hair that hung well past the collar of a black leather jacket. Dark jeans clung to thighs that were as thick as cannon barrels.

The man nudged Ivan's shoulder. "If these jackshits expect you to work twenty-four seven, they're not paying you enough."

"If I work twenty-four seven, I'll finish my degree, get out of this place, and finally make decent money. Then I'll be able to take a vacation with you." Ivan locked his door, turned, and spotted her. A flush rushed up his neck and turned his ears a deep, plum red. "Tia, I'd like you to meet my brother, Victor. He stopped by on his way to Killington."

The man turned toward her. He possessed the same heavy bone structure as Ivan, along with the deep chest and brawny arms. After a long look at her, he opened one large hand in a brief wave.

"Hi." She sniffled to ward off the hard sting inside her nose. Any second now, big drips of silent tears would roll out of her nostrils. Aware of a murmur of deep voices as both men walked toward her, she fumbled with her keys to unlock the doorknob. Desperate not to break down into ugly sobs in the middle of the hallway, she stepped into her apartment and gave her door a quick shove.

It closed halfway, thudded against something, and swung open.

Ivan stepped into the threshold and looked over his

shoulder. "I'll talk to you later, Vic."

Tia hung up her coat in a dim attempt to act like she wasn't upset, but her nose didn't cooperate. A hot drip rolled out of her nostril. She grabbed a tissue and pressed it against her nose. Everything inside her ached, but she didn't want to cry. She hated crying out of her nostrils. It was weird and gross.

The door closed with a quiet thud.

"You're sniffling." Ivan moved close to her. "What's wrong?"

"Rough day." She wadded the wet tissue in her hand and sniffled again.

"Here." A clean tissue dangled from his blunt fingertips.

Always paying attention, this man. She wiped off another drip from her nose.

"Talk to me." He placed a hand on her hip. "I want to know what happened, please."

The please got to her. He was the only one who used that word when he asked for something.

"I said the wrong thing to one of my clients and n-now she can't stand me." A sob blasted out of the tight, painful spot in her chest. She pressed her hands over her thumping heart and looked up at Ivan. "This whole thing is my f-fault, and there's nothing I can do to change what h-happened. I feel awful about what I did."

"I know. I can tell." He unzipped his coat with one urgent yank and pulled her into a warm hug. "I've got you now. Not letting go 'til you feel better."

Nestled against his chest, she felt protected. Accepted, too, in spite of what she'd done. Maybe because of that, she began to cry. Tears rolled out of her eyes, turning her cheeks slick. With her face pressed against the column of Ivan's warm neck, she cried like she used to, when she didn't have to be strong all the time.

It felt good to let go.

After a short while, she felt better. Her mistake hadn't been rectified, but she was in Ivan's arms and that made all the difference.

He spread his hands along her back as though he needed to touch as much of her as possible. "I want to know what you're thinking. Can you tell me?"

"My client needed me to trust her judgment, to believe her, and I didn't," she admitted, swallowing another sob. "I let my past get in the way of how I listened, of how I reacted."

"I do the same thing. There are times when my past bleeds into how I act, what I say." Ivan kissed her temple, his words warm and forgiving against her skin. "It's gonna be okay."

She didn't deserve such tender care from him, because she was just like the therapist who'd hurt him so deeply. She hadn't listened. She'd formed opinions about Pamela's boyfriend without speaking to Greg, without hearing his side of the story. Feeling guilty, she bit down on her bottom lip. "I drew the wrong conclusions. I assumed things that weren't true. I stopped listening. I don't know how to fix this, Ivan."

He wiped the tears off her cheek with a slow sweep of his thumb. "Maybe all you need to do is start listening again. To yourself. Trust your instincts. You're smart enough to recognize when the past is horning in on the present. You'll find a way to turn those memories into strengths. You'll turn things around."

A shiver skimmed across her aching heart. Grateful for his faith in her, she rose onto her toes and hugged Ivan around the shoulders, stroking the impressive width of his upper back. "I'm so glad you're here."

"Feels good," he murmured against her damp cheek. "*You* feel good. In my arms and in my mind. For the first time in my life, I'm with a woman who makes me happy, even when she cries."

Wow, okay. That was a spectacular thing to say. All the sharp edges of her bad day blurred. Ivan was here, his rock-hard body crowding away her loneliness. She cupped the sturdy column of his neck and kissed him, going dizzy the instant her lips touched his.

His big body tightened, yet his mouth softened in immediate welcome.

A phone rang.

"Damn. Whoever wants to talk can wait." He reached into his coat pocket to silence the call and kissed his way back to her mouth.

The phone blared again.

"I'll turn off my phone," Ivan growled.

"No, you'd better answer the call. It might be important if they keep calling."

He yanked the phone up to his ear. "Hey, Smitty. What's up?" Ivan listened for a moment and exhaled. "I'm not sure when I'll get back to the lab, so try isolating the new code and text me if that doesn't work." He shoved the phone into his pocket and put his arms back around her. "I'm not going anywhere until I know you're okay."

"I'm fine, really." She pulled in a watery breath and tried to smile.

"No, I'm not buying that." He strengthened his hold around her waist. "I heard another sniffle."

"Yes, because you're not leaving until I'm okay and that's making me want to cry again. Please go back to the lab so I don't burst into another ugly crying jag." She touched his jaw, unable to resist all of that whiskery goodness. "I'm fine. I'm going to go to yoga class with Annette, and then I'm going out to dinner with you."

"I'll pick you up at six-thirty. I'm paying for the meal, Miss Self-Sufficient, so don't bring your wallet."

She opened her mouth to protest.

He silenced her with a firm kiss and walked out of her apartment.

Without all of his fierce energy filling up the space, her living room felt hollow and cold. That emptiness made her feel like a fraud, because she was doing exactly what she didn't want any other woman to do.

She was beginning to need a man, and he was leaving in a few short weeks.

CHAPTER TWELVE

Ivan caught a whiff of antiseptic and fought the urge to barf. God, this couldn't be happening. An hour ago, everything was going so well. He'd fixed the glitch in the Aurora software in time to get ready for his date with Tia. Then his cell phone rang and everything went to shit.

Now he couldn't fix a thing. All he could do was wait in the hospital, where suffering clung to the walls the same way tattered address labels clung to old magazine covers. A constant barrage of bad news gushed from the waiting room's television. Anxiety crawled up his spine on soggy knees, leaving behind cold splotches of sweat.

He'd spent too much time watching his mother suffer while she'd battled cancer. Now he sat helplessly in some crappy room while his brother suffered in surgery.

Ivan checked the time. Six-twenty. He should call Tia and tell her he wasn't going to show up, but his throat was so tight he could barely talk. A text would have to do.

MountainMan: I'm at the hospital. My brother was in a car accident. It's bad. He's in surgery, now. I'll be here for most of the night.

Three dots appeared on the screen as she typed her response.

Boots: You're doing the right thing. Take care of your brother and call if you need me.

***

Six hours later, Ivan sprawled on his mattress. Nothing but black shadows surrounded him. No big deal. He was used to the hollow silence this late at night.

He stared at the ceiling but his mind wouldn't rest. His interview with Phoros was in a couple of days, but he couldn't leave Victor. The visit to Boston would have to wait. Everything would wait until his brother got better. That's the only thing that mattered.

All Vic needed was time. He'd get through this. Hell, he'd survived deployments in the worst armpits of the Middle East. A car accident wouldn't stop him.

Ivan rolled to his side and stared at his closet. Somewhere on the other side of that wall was Tia. Was one-thirty in the morning too late to talk? Yes, definitely, but she'd told him to call if he needed her. So he reached for his glasses and grabbed his phone.

Tia answered on the second ring. "Hi. How's your brother?"

"Not good." Ivan edged his glasses down so he could rub the tight spot on the bridge of his nose. "All of this

153

damned snow turned the highway into a skating rink. Vic must've skidded on some ice and slid off the road into a ditch. A branch pierced the windshield and ripped his face. The ER doctors had to call in a plastic surgeon to sew up the lacerations. Three hundred stitches, give or take."

"Oh, Ivan."

The soft, sympathetic way she said his name made him feel like he wasn't so alone. "There's a bad scratch on his cornea. They think he might lose the sight in his left eye. We won't know for a few days."

"I'm sure the doctors will do everything they can to help him."

There was no spit in Ivan's mouth to swallow past the knot of fear stuck in his throat. "They put Victor in ICU. They won't let me stay with him. I don't know what to do."

Sheets rustled on Tia's end of the phone. "Are you still at the hospital?"

"No, I'm in my apartment." He scanned his dim bedroom. All he had was a queen-sized mattress on a cheap metal frame. No headboard, no footboard, just a set of white sheets and a quilt, yet this bed looked like a king's compared to Victor's hospital cot.

"I'm coming over." A click ended the call, followed by the dial tone.

Ivan dropped the phone and shoved the quilt aside. He sprinted toward his door dressed in nothing but a pair of boxer shorts. A rough tremble turned his hands into useless things. Took him three tries to turn the lock. He flung open the door with one desperate yank.

Tia stood there in a plain, dark nightie. The vee neck displayed a generous hint of her full breasts and the short hem skimmed her upper thighs as she held up her phone. "I had to bring this because the on-call therapist might need backup. Want some company?"

He hauled her into his arms.

She kissed his cheek and combed cool fingers through his hair.

Those caresses broke him, made him confess everything. "I should've made Vic stay until the storm eased up. If I'd taken him to the lab with me, he wouldn't have gotten into that accident. He'd be in Killington and not in some hospital bed."

"If you'd delayed him, he would've gotten on the road later. The highway might've been slicker. His accident might've been worse."

True. He hadn't thought of that, but still. "I haven't seen Vic in months. Why'd I blow him off?"

"Because you had work to do. He seemed to understand."

"He was in a ditch for who knows how long. If someone hadn't spotted his car..." Ivan couldn't bear to think of Victor trapped in the wreck, alone and bleeding.

"He's safe now. Drat, let me get rid of my phone and key so I can hold you better." She placed her things on the card table and pulled him back into her arms.

Felt so good. He pressed his cheek against hers, not caring when his glasses went askew. "One side of his face is all wrapped up. They had to sedate him so he wouldn't tear off the bandages."

"They'll take good care of him."

"I want to take care of him. I owe him that. He's the one who took care of me when my mother had cancer."

Tia's hands stopped stroking across his back. "Cancer?"

"Stage Three breast cancer. I was in seventh grade when she went through surgery and chemo. My Dad would work all day and spend all night at the hospital. My brother, Gabe, was overseas. Victor was the only one at home. He was in high school, right in the middle of football season. After practice, he'd cook me dinner even though he was dead on his feet. I was clueless in the kitchen. Couldn't even make a can of soup. Still can't."

A startled laugh came out of her. She hugged him tight and looked up at him. "Tell me more."

"For three months, we didn't know if Mom would live or die. I stopped studying. Stopped eating. Stopped talking. Didn't care about anything." And his anger grew, a quivering, violent thing he couldn't control. He spent hours in the driveway, pelting a hockey puck into the weathered goal in front of their garage. "Victor was the only one who saw my fear. He quit football, which meant he gave up the chance for a scholarship, and stayed close to home. Rather than catch passes, Vic caught me. He made sure I did my homework, drove me to ice hockey practice, watched every practice, every game. He was my rock while Mom recovered. Now he's in trouble. This is my chance to take care of him, but the damned nurses won't let me stay by his side."

"You'll be able to stay with him in a day or two. Right now, the nurses need to keep a close eye on him without his big, well-meaning brother getting in the way." She stroked the back of his neck, her palm a welcome balm against his skin.

The caress rolled a pleasant shiver down his spine. He inhaled a gulp of the sweet smell of her. The thin fabric of her nightie was more of a tease than a barrier between her lush breasts and his bare chest. He slid his hand down to her lower back until he got near the sexy curve of her butt.

The Mountain Man inside him awoke. He wanted to grab her stellar ass and bury himself deep inside her warmth, but any second now she'd take stock of his barren apartment and realize he didn't have any furniture. She'd begin to piece together how far he'd fallen.

Eight months ago, one brittle moment had stripped away most of his belongings and all of his pride. He'd let anger and frustration get to him, proof he wasn't so smart after all.

He peeled his hands off her and stepped back so she could get a good look at nothing. No couch, no television, no pictures on the wall. No kitchen table, no shelves, no books except for the computer engineering texts stacked beside the old card table that served as his desk. The folding chair was a cast-off he'd found in a dumpster.

If he'd had anything in his stomach, he would've felt nauseated. Situation normal. He'd done a damned fine job of hiding his poverty, but his empty living room made him feel stripped bare, exposed. Any second now, Tia would ask why he didn't have any furniture. He didn't want to admit that nearly every penny of his disposable income had gone toward lawyer's fees to expunge his ex-girlfriend's restraining order.

Tia glanced around. "Your desk is immaculate. That's the most precise stack of textbooks I've ever seen. And look, your boots are lined up next to your sneakers in a straight row by the door. I'm having a moment, here. You're a neat-freak's dream come true, you know that?"

"What?" He had next to nothing, yet this woman didn't see the hollow emptiness. Instead, she saw the careful way he treated the few things he had. A thin stream of hope spurted inside him. "Wait 'til you see my closet. There's not a stitch of clothing out of place."

"Oh, wow. You're singing the song of my people." She waved a hand near her face. "I feel a little flushed."

He chuckled, grateful for the moment of levity. Now that he was with her, he felt a helluva lot better. "I know it's the middle of the night, but could you stay for a while?"

"Of course."

He held out his hand and savored the way she laced her fingers through his in absolute trust. Wanting to preserve that trust, he offered her a choice and a promise. "We can stay in the living room or sit on my bed. With either option, you'll be safe with me."

To her credit, she didn't make a snide remark about the lack of furniture in his empty living room. "Your bed sounds good. We can talk, there."

"Fine, then." He led her to the bedroom and turned on the small lamp that sat on the box he used as a nightstand. "Settle down on this side so you won't feel the draft from the window." He tucked his only pillow behind her so she'd be comfortable and sat beside her, content to lean back against the cold wall as long as Tia was next to him. She was shivering, though. He tugged the quilt over her legs, which was a crying shame. Nothing should cover those perfect legs.

She lifted the edge of the quilt to take a closer look. "Is this pink?"

"Yeah. My aunt made the quilt for me. She's eighty years old and likes bright fabrics."

"Oh. Well, there's nothing better than a homemade quilt from someone who loves you." Tia patted the bright fabric as though the garish colors created a beautiful combination. "I have a quilt, too. From my abuela. It's blue. My favorite color."

Yet she didn't wear a speck of blue. Just black and white. Those neutral colors made her confession seem more profound, as though she didn't reveal many personal things to many people.

"You seem worried about Victor staying in the ICU. Can you tell me why?"

"Anesthesia doesn't sit well with him. Makes him unpredictable." Ivan cracked a knuckle and thought of his brother, dazed by drugs and pain. "Before I left the hospital, I gave my number to every nurse on duty. I warned them that Victor doesn't react well to pain medications, but everyone seemed to think there wouldn't be a problem."

"Okay. Do you know the extent of his injuries?"

"Possible concussion. A couple of bruised ribs. Cuts on his face, neck, and chest. The plastic surgeon said the gash on Vic's face goes from eyebrow to lip. The doctor tried to close the laceration as best as he could, but there will be a scar. There's also a chance the injury severed a nerve, which means the left side of Victor's face might droop. We won't know until the bandages are removed."

"When will that be?"

"A few days." He took a deep breath and tried not to think of everything that could go wrong. "One nurse claimed he'd be just fine, but I know that's a lie. Even if Vic manages to keep the vision in his injured eye, his life will never be the same. That scar will change the way he looks, the way he lives. Whenever anyone sees his face, they'll ask what happened to him. He'll have to relive his car accident over and over."

Sympathy rose in her gaze. "You're right. I hadn't thought of that."

"That's what happened with the scar on my chin. Before I grew a beard, everyone wanted to know how I got hurt. I didn't like to admit that I wasn't quick enough to avoid getting hit in the face with a hockey puck." Ivan rubbed that spot on his chin, able to feel the nasty scar beneath his whiskers. "If people constantly ask Victor about the scar on his face, he won't want to explain. Vic doesn't like to talk about himself." Ivan glanced toward his closet, able to see the flannel shirt he'd borrowed from Victor a few months ago. The sleeves were way too long. "My brother is a big guy. The sheer size of him makes people think twice about approaching him. The scar will make him look like he's some brute who enjoys kicking ass, but that's not true. He takes care of people. He'd do anything for…"

Grief smothered the rest of his words. He wiped a hand across his throbbing eyes.

"You love him so much," Tia whispered.

"Yeah. Bone deep." He hated the fear that scraped the underside of his skin. He couldn't afford to be scared. "Victor is the one person who gave me what I needed when I was too terrified to ask for help. Now he's the one in trouble. I need to be strong for him. I'm all he has right now."

"Where is the rest of your family?"

"My parents are in Slovakia visiting family, and my other brother is on vacation in Hawaii with his wife. They're all scrambling to fly home, but they're having trouble finding flights." Ivan winced, thinking of the brief glimpse he'd gotten of Victor's face wrapped in gauze. "I can't lose it when I see Victor's scar. I don't want my brother to think he's anything less than perfect to me. If I can't pull myself together, how can I help him get through this?"

"You don't have to pull yourself together. You can feel scared and worried and sick to your stomach. You can even break down and cry while you're with him." She squeezed Ivan's hand. "He needs *you*. Just as you are. Believe me, you're more than enough."

"God, Tia." He gave into the urgent need inside him and rolled toward her.

CHAPTER THIRTEEN

When the sun knitted milky threads of daylight into the bedroom, Tia woke up. Her head was pillowed on a firm shoulder. The front of her was cuddled against a warm side. Her hand rested on a bare, broad chest. The hair that grew there reminded her of the way her aunt's terrier used to feel, coarse and springy. But Ivan was no small pet. He was a long slab of muscle that took up most of the bed.

He lay flat on his back, staring at the ceiling. Aside from the steady rise and fall of his chest, he was as still as stone, a slab of granite that could have been mined from the mountains surrounding campus. His mouth formed a tight, straight line within the lush shadow of his beard. A deep pinch pulled at the outer corner of his eyes.

She could read him, now. Ivan was worried. Heartsick. And he hadn't slept much at all.

"Hi," she whispered.

He turned his head to look at her. "Mornin.'"

"I fell asleep," she admitted, feeling guilty. "I meant to stay awake with you."

"That's all right." He put his hand on top of hers, the movement slow and solemn.

"Now you can say I slept with you on our first date," she teased, wanting to coax a smile out of him. "I also slept with you before then. In handcuffs."

"Last night meant more. You were here because you wanted to be with me, not because a pair of manacles trapped you." Sincerity glowed from his bright blue eyes, his voice deep and husky. "You knew I needed you. I didn't even have to ask."

And soon after she'd stepped into his apartment, he'd brought her to his bed because that was the only piece of decent furniture he had, gave her the only pillow he had, and opened up about the worries he had. When he'd finally reached for her, his big body was rigid and cold. She'd pulled the quilt over him and rubbed his back until he relaxed in her arms. She'd felt so needed, and so safe, that she snuggled against him and fell asleep.

Now the almond scent of him was all around her, toasty and tempting. She was in bed with Mountain Man, who was rock-boned with so many hills of muscle. She swept a soft caress against his chest, liking the way his body hair tickled her fingertips.

Ivan dropped his gaze to the neckline of her nightie and then turned his head to resume staring at the ceiling. A red flush stalked across his cheek and bled into the shell of his ear. He released her hand and dug his fingers into the quilt.

Well, drat. She was barely dressed and he wasn't going to make a move on her.

Then again, he was barely dressed and she wasn't making a move on him, either.

Tossing the quilt aside, she swung one leg over his hips and planted her knees on either side of his hips. Her breasts swung beneath her silky camisole slip, a sultry reminder she wasn't wearing a bra. She didn't want to wear anything at all, but first she had to convince Ivan that she didn't want him to act like a gentleman.

His gaze locked on hers, his dark eyebrows two harsh slashes beneath a frown. The dim morning sun highlighted the blond and copper whiskers within his beard. The skin across the bridge of his nose contained a ruddy glow. This man was a tapestry of color, from the bright blue of his eyes to the warm copper and gold in his beard.

She loved looking at the rich hues of Ivan Antonov.

"I might go for your cheek first," she told him. "Kind of a safe bet to start there."

"Start what?"

"Kissing you." She pressed her lips against his sturdy cheekbone. His skin was warm, the texture thick. She nuzzled her way along the silky-stiff whiskers that grew all over his jaw. Not a trace of hair product or aftershave altered the nutty taste of him, just pure Ivan. Once she got to the firm curve of his bottom lip, she stayed there. "I won't stop until you feel better."

Two divots formed on either side of his mouth, happy

dimples within his thick coat of whiskers. "You touch me and I want to burn that feeling into my brain. You light me up. Everything about you, Tia. Just...everything."

She leaned on the hard curve of his shoulders, pinning his remarkable body to the mattress so she could do whatever she wanted for as long as she wanted. A soft lick along his lips parted his mouth. She dipped her tongue inside to taste him. His flavor made her breath stop and heart pound.

His big hands slid up her thighs until his blunt fingertips dipped under the thin hem of her nightie. "I dream of you. Of this. Every single night."

Shivers ran up the inside of her thighs. Needing to rub against something, she lowered her hips to his. His cock was a thick, long ridge beneath his boxers. She glided against him, her body going wet against that impressive hardness. She could probably climax just by rocking against this sturdy man.

He kissed a path down her throat. When he got to a spot near her collarbone, his kiss turned into a sexy lick.

"Oh, I like that." She shivered.

"Me, too." He grinned. "Been wondering how you'd react if I kissed this little triangle of freckles on your skin."

"Now you know." Happiness beamed into her, as bright as a sunrise. She pulled off her camisole and stretched out on top of him. The crinkly hairs on his chest stroked her breasts and tickled her nipples. Everything inside her jumped and curled.

He groaned and locked an arm around her, rolling until he was on his side, facing her. "Tia Garcia. Your name is a poem to me, your touch is a miracle to me."

Her mind stuttered. "A miracle?"

"There's no other way to explain how you affect me." He cupped her breast, his touch gentle. "You make me think of sonnets."

"Sonnets?" Tia touched his jaw, surprised by this romantic side of him.

He skimmed his thumb near her nipple, his touch reverent. "Shakespeare said it best. 'For all this, each hand, each finger, each lip, each breath, each sigh, each word and sound of voice or tongue, I would require an age to contemplate.' In other words, you fascinate me."

"Shakespeare should be illegal." Because then she'd have the perfect excuse to handcuff Ivan again.

"I had to read a few sonnets in college. Didn't see the value in them until now." He gazed down at her breast as his hand curled around that curve. "It's a holy thing to be able to touch you. If a verse convinces you of that fact, I'm saying it." He lowered his head to the puckered peak of her nipple, his kiss as slow as honey on a cold morning.

Everything he did was gentle. Careful. Thoughtful. Tia didn't want that. She wanted her Mountain Man with all of his rough edges, so she slid both hands into his thick hair to keep him close to her breast. "Suck it, please."

He pulled the tip into his mouth, the flat of his tongue soft against her flesh.

Felt good, but not quite right. This was nothing like the kiss he'd given her the other night, when he'd lost all control and went after her with everything he had. She liked that raw, unedited version of Ivan but didn't know how to get him there.

One look at the bedrock of muscle across his wide shoulders and all she wanted to do was suck on all that strength. Jeez, his deltoids were twice the size of her hands. She caressed those round muscles and sighed. Or whimpered. Okay, both.

Ivan lifted his head. "What's wrong?"

"I'm losing my mind." She trailed a caress down his broad back, slowing down as she reached his waist. She pulled her hand toward his front, coasting her palm along a sturdy abdomen bricked with muscle. "Every single part of you is rock hard."

And all hers to explore. She nibbled her way down his neck, pausing near the bulge of his Adam's apple to discover the faint rasp of fresh whiskers that had sprouted overnight. Near the base of his throat, she found a bare spot with no whiskers at all. The skin was smooth, a perfect place to lick.

Ivan jerked.

She kept going, dropping kisses on his hairy chest, loving the way those crisp hairs felt against her lips. His nipple was the only thing he possessed that was smaller than hers. She touched the little nub with the tip of her tongue.

He grabbed her arm. "Let me make you feel good."

"Shh. I'm having a moment, here." Her breath raised goose bumps across his flesh. She traced those bumps with her lips and returned to his nipple. She kissed that tiny round bump the way she wanted that part of her to be kissed. First soft, then wet, then finishing off with a lusty suck to make everything hard and tingly.

"*God.*"

She smiled against his chest and moved her hand along his sturdy side. Her fingertips bumped into the ribbed elastic waistband of his boxers, so close to the ass she'd never handled. She stopped breathing.

So did he.

The bed spun. So did her head. She forced her lungs to pull in some oxygen and some of the dizziness cleared. She kissed the center of his chest and felt his heart thump against her lips like a drum in a rock anthem. Driven by that fast beat, she moved her hand a little bit lower and remembered the time she'd seen him lift free weights in the gym, seen his sweat-drenched shorts, seen his butt flex as he squatted three hundred pounds. Now that she had that formidable curve of muscle within her grasp, she felt fierce. Primal. Ready to take what she wanted. She curled her fingers around that brawny ass and squeezed.

"You." He thrust a hand into her hair, his grip urgent. "*This.*"

Whenever Ivan went monosyllabic, good things happened. She nibbled on him, loving the combination of warm lips and cool beard. "You're a gorgeous man. Have I ever said? Because, really, you're stunning in so many ways."

His mouth opened, parting her lips to sweep his tongue inside, hot and insistent. He flattened his chest on hers, sending shivers across her breasts as though his skin was charged with electricity. The firm globes of his ass flexed under her hands. The thick length of his cock pressed against her, pulling her satin panties tight across her sex.

Pleasure zinged between her legs, hot and tingly. "If you keep kissing me like this, I'll come."

"Making you come is what I fucking live for."

That was definitely unedited. He'd never dropped an f-bomb until now. Her Mountain Man was back, breathing hard and shoving the quilt off the bed. His elbow bumped into the wall with a loud whack.

She winced. "Are you hurt?"

"Yeah. Dying. For you." His hand curled around her hip, his gaze blazing. "Tee?"

"Yes." She squirmed out of her panties and almost cried out when the blunt tip of his finger grazed the lips of her sex.

A lush, hot clench rippled into her lower belly. A seductive heaviness settled low in her abdomen, forming a pool of warm, lovely heat. She closed her eyes and knew this wouldn't take long. Every part of her body vibrated, ready for release. The primitive need on Ivan's face was almost enough to send her over the edge.

Every part of him bulged, coiled tight and trembling, everything but his hand, which was sure and steady and slow, drifting across her like a soft breeze on a summer day. That loving stroke enticed her to open up more, arch into him, silently beg for a little bit more. He gave it, over and over, tempting touches that invited her to trust him, pledged to keep her safe, promised to give her what she needed, sheltering her with his big body as his fingers stroked and caressed as he leaned down to take the tip of her breast in his mouth. First soft, then wet, and finishing off with a hard lusty suck.

That suck triggered her orgasm, zinging quick pulses that vibrated into her, a surprise and a relief. She stretched into the feeling, curling her toes as the climax peaked and faded. Out of breath but satisfied, she relaxed into a grin.

"Hell, no. You're not done, yet." He curled his hand around her thigh. "I'm giving you more than that."

She laughed. "What could possibly be better than a climax?"

"A better climax. The Big O. An orgasm that'll prove my worth." He pulled her leg over his hip. A sexy smile coasted across his mouth. "I want to give a self-sufficient woman like you reason to come back for more."

"Believe me, you've done a thorough job already." But his finger felt good gliding across the swollen flesh of her sex.

"Just wait, honey." He slid two thick fingers into her core.

Those fingers touched places that welcomed the attention. She squirmed a bit when he got to a spot that couldn't seem to handle both of his fingers.

"You're tight right here. More snug." He groaned as if he was the one about to come undone. "In other words, you're perfect."

She squirmed a little bit, liking the way he felt inside her, liking the way he stared down at her, liking the husky growl in his voice.

"You, in my bed. Me, wrapped all around you. Us, together." He kissed the corner of her mouth. "You call me Mountain Man and I feel as strong as granite." He nipped at her lip. "You touch me and I want nothing else." He nudged his fingers a bit deeper into her and touched something that made her body jolt. "Looks like I found what I was looking for." He moved his finger again.

It was too much and not enough. She moaned.

"I'll remember this, Boots." Dark promise turned his voice into a low purr. "If you ask me to make love to you, I'll angle my hips and aim for this narrow spot that makes you burn."

"I'm close. I'm falling apart. Don't stop." She gripped his shoulder, which was tight and hot, the same way she felt right now.

The buildup to a climax was always her favorite part about sex, and that feeling started to build. She wished he'd plunge those fingers deeper and prayed he wouldn't, so turned on she forgot to breathe. Finally, he rubbed the palm of his hand against her clit and everything inside her coiled tighter.

"*Ivan*." The push of his fingers inside her produced a tingling throb and his palm against her clit coaxed a high zing. The two sensations tugged and pulled, over and over, twining a ribbon of pleasure higher and higher until her entire body shook.

His hot gaze swept down to where his hand was between her legs. "This, Tee. You and me. This is what I need."

Her climax exploded. White stars popped across her vision. Pleasure surged deep and made her a mindless thing, bucking against his hand as her sex sucked on his fingers.

"Good lord, I can feel your body pulling me in deeper." Chest heaving, he swooped down for a kiss as he stroked his fingers into her.

The orgasm kept going, so intense she cried out against his mouth. When the mind-bending pleasure finally diminished, she dug her fingers into his hair and sighed. "Never in my life has sex been this good. I think I heard angels sing."

"The choir is just getting started." He took a breast in one hand, cupped an ass cheek in the other, and planted a hot kiss on her neck.

Something buzzed. She didn't want to pay attention to that noise, but she had a bad feeling the hospital was calling Ivan.

It buzzed again, muffled but insistent, somewhere below them.

"I think your phone is ringing." She glanced at the wad of tangled bedding on the floor. "Sounds like it's somewhere under the quilt."

"Shit." He lunged, found his phone, and sat on the edge of the bed.

When the nurse on the other end of the phone began to speak, she was loud enough for Tia to hear. Victor hadn't done well after the anesthesia wore off. He'd vomited eleven times overnight and was having trouble with the painkillers. They'd move him into a private room once he calmed down. The nurse asked when Ivan might arrive.

"I'll head over now." Ivan hung up, his eyebrows pulled together in a grim line. "I'm sorry, Tia. I need to go."

"I know." She settled beside him and placed her hand along the back of his neck. That spot was flat and warm but the muscles beneath were bunched taut. "Call if you need anything, okay?"

He nodded and started to get dressed.

Seeing him shirtless in a pair of jeans was something to behold. That broad, hairy chest narrowed to chiseled abs that flexed when he pulled a fresh shirt over his head. Tia tried not to drool as she shimmied into her panties, put her nightie back on, and heard her phone ping. And ping. And ping.

That couldn't be good. No one texted her this early in the morning.

She went into the living room to check her phone. Three text messages appeared on the screen.

WHoover: We need to talk. Right now. Are you awake?

WHoover: I talked to someone in The Women's Grid. She knows some things about your neighbor. Bad things.

WHoover: His ex slapped a restraining order against him cuz he's a raging alcoholic. Stay away from that heartless asshole.

This couldn't be true. Ivan wasn't the type of man who'd hit someone. Weeks ago, he'd gone out of his way to avoid slamming a volleyball at anyone during their intramural game. That carefulness extended outside of the gym, too. Whenever she'd been with him, she'd felt safe. There were times when his touch was urgent, but never violent.

She'd never seen him with a drink in his hand, never seen him drunk. The one time she'd offered him a beer, he'd turned it down. At the time, she'd assumed he was sticking to a clean diet, which might not be right. Had he refused to take the beer because he had a problem with alcohol? Did he get aggressive when he drank? Had she misread him?

Her confidence wobbled like the first wisp of steam from a teakettle.

Ivan stopped beside her. "I'll call you, later."

"Wait. Read this." She showed him the text.

His gaze went as flat as the hard line of his mouth. "Who sent that?"

"Wayne did, just now. He saw me with you on Saturday night, when we walked into town." But she couldn't walk now. Her legs trembled on knees that had locked in place while she tried to sort fact from fiction. She pointed to the damning message on her phone. "Did someone file a restraining order against you?"

"Yeah. My ex-girlfriend did."

Everything seemed to stop. Her breath. Her heart. Her blood. "Why?"

"Because she thought I was heartless. Her therapist agreed with her." He shoved his keys into his pocket. "The charges were dismissed. A judge found no probable cause to enforce the restraining order. I've spent every last dime on lawyers' fees to clear my name, but that hasn't stopped The Women's Grid from dragging me through the dirt."

"I don't understand. What happened?"

He stopped moving. "Didn't you hear what I said? The court cleared my name. They dropped the charges because there was no reason to believe I posed a threat. Nothing in that text from your so-called friend is true. It's all rumors and lies."

Now she was really confused. "You just said your ex filed a restraining order, so isn't that part true?"

A flush turned his face a deep scarlet. "Do you really want to do this now? I have to go to the hospital, dammit."

She flinched and clasped her phone, her hands shaky and damp. "Please don't yell. I know you need to go see your brother. We can talk later. I want to hear your side of the story."

"Fine." He didn't sound fine at all. He sounded livid. Looked it, too, as he yanked his coat off a hook and flung open the door.

The hall's bright fluorescent light hurt Tia's eyes as she walked out. The floor was cold against her bare feet and the thin hem of her satin nightie tickled her thighs with every quick step toward her apartment. Fortunately, no one was around to see her dressed in next to nothing with her hair a tangled mess, but this still felt like a walk of shame. She'd rolled around in bed with Ivan even though she knew very little about him, and now she'd just found out that his ex, and her therapist, and people in The Grid thought he didn't have a heart.

She paused to look at him as he walked past.

His icy blue eyes didn't go anywhere near her.

In that bleak moment, she couldn't see his heart, either.

Chapter Fourteen

Ivan took a deep breath through his mouth so he wouldn't get a nose full of hospital smells. He should've been used to the scent of disinfectant after spending the past three days at Manchester General, but every whiff brought back memories of his mother at her weakest. And now Victor.

His brother was too big for the hospital bed. Both of his feet hung over the edge of the mattress, which couldn't be comfortable. A blue gown stretched across a ribcage that was still breathing, thank God. The big guy hadn't bathed in days, so his hair was a long knotted tangle, but that was okay, because Vic looked like Vic.

Yeah, a long row of stitches laced up a vicious laceration along the side of his face and a white patch of gauze covered his left eye, but the cut hadn't severed the nerves in Vic's face. Nothing sagged.

Well, nothing except this heinous chair. Ivan shifted,

trying to get comfortable in a seat that had less padding than an old gurney.

Victor's right eye opened. For the first time since the accident, his gaze was sharp enough to zoom in on Ivan's rumpled shirt. "Looks like you crawled out of a rucksack."

Ivan shrugged. "I'm going for a casual look."

"Casual, my ass. You've been with me ever since I left the I.C.U."

"Damn right, and I'll be here until you walk out of this place."

"Don't you have something better to do, like finish your degree?"

"I've managed to get some work done on my laptop while you snore like old Uncle Bronislav."

"No one snores like Bronislav." Victor shoved a greasy hank of hair off his face. "What day is it?"

"Friday."

Victor's nostrils flared on a low, angry snarl. "Aren't you s'posed to be in Boston for that interview?"

"We discussed this six hours ago." Ivan waved a hand to dismiss the topic. "You don't remember a thing when you're on painkillers."

"Isn't that the point? The best time to smear gunk on a guy's eye is when he's looped."

"Are you saying that you'd rather get poked in the eye while you're sober?"

"Answer me. Why aren't you in Boston?"

"Because I didn't want to go. No big deal." The visit to Phoros had fallen on the same day the specialist was supposed to examine Victor, so Ivan stuck around.

Victor produced a one-eyed glare. "Reschedule the interview."

"No can do. Phoros already offered the job to someone else, but that doesn't matter. I've accepted an offer from a different firm. I'll be in their research and development department, which is what I wanted to do." Not entirely, but he'd be gainfully employed. With the money he'd earn, he could rebuild his life, maybe even buy a few luxuries like a high-def TV.

For now, though, he was content to watch the mediocre television in his brother's hospital room. "Believe it or not, this place gets a ton of sports channels. I've been watching a lot of hockey. The Bruins are winning, by the way. Their losing streak is about to end."

"Miracles do happen." Victor sat up and swung one hairy leg out of the bed.

Ivan leaned forward, ready to stop another attempted escape. "Where are you going?"

"To take a leak." Victor swung his other leg over the edge of the bed.

"Here, take my hand."

"Back off. I can walk to the fucking john." Victor slapped both bare feet on the tile floor, stood, and turned a terrifying shade of gray.

Ivan grabbed him. "Get back into bed if you're gonna pass out, dammit."

"Screw that." Vic took a step. And another.

"Take it easy. We've got a short way to go and long time to get there." Ivan kept a firm grip on Victor's waist like he'd been doing for the past few days, but this was the first time his brother was sober enough to know he couldn't get around on his own.

Vic swatted at Ivan's hand. "Back off."

The terse order hurt more than the swat. Ivan let go but remained close in case his brother took a nosedive.

Didn't happen. Vic moved toward the toilet and lifted the front of his gown. A thick stream of urine hit the water. Even though he'd been hospitalized for days, had a couple of bruised ribs, and too many cuts to count, he stood tall and straight. Like a Marine. A big one. Six feet, eight inches, two-hundred ninety pounds of muscle and bone, square-jawed and formidable.

The back of Ivan's throat stung with awe.

Vic walked back without any help and sank into the hospital bed.

Ivan flopped into The Heinous Chair. "Do you remember what happened the night of your accident?"

"Talking won't change what happened." Victor stared at the television.

"Still, I'd like to know. How much snow was on the road?"

All that got was a grunt.

"How fast were you going?"

One shoulder lifted.

"Was traffic heavy?"

Nothing.

Conversation over. Victor always clammed up about things that pained him. His ability to carry a burden had served him well. After four years of deployment in the Marines, he'd emerged with just one scar, a squiggly one on his chest, but he never talked about the weird mark.

Every Antonov buried their feelings in order to get things done. That's what Ivan did, too. He stuffed all the hurt and pain deep inside because whenever he let those emotions boil over, everything went to hell.

Like a few days ago, when he'd yelled at Tia.

A hard throb pinged against the inside of his skull. Another headache. He felt like a big puddle of moose piss. He leaned back in The Heinous Chair and looked at his brother, who probably felt worse than he did. "Mom and Dad are flying in tomorrow. Gabe and Leigh, too."

Victor rolled his eye. "Tell them to stay put. I don't want everyone hovering around me as if I'm about to die."

"You almost did, which is why everyone is freaking out. If you don't want family around, tell them yourself."

Vic's hand opened. "Give me your cell."

"No. Get your own phone."

"Never gonna happen." Vic kept his hand out, waiting.

"Drives me crazy that you're so hard to reach. If you had a cell phone—"

"You found me just fine."

"Because I have a cell phone, damn it." Ivan slapped the phone into Vic's palm.

Victor proceeded to call Dad, which was a brilliant move. Mom would've been a much tougher nut to crack.

Ivan listened to his brother list all of the reasons why he didn't need help. Sure, he had a few scrapes but he was fine. The hospital would discharge him, soon. He'd stay in Vermont for a couple of days and then head home. Victor insisted that he'd feel "guilty as all hell" if Mom and Dad cut short the only big vacation they'd taken in the past five years. He urged Dad to stay in Slovakia until Mom had the chance to visit Uncle Bronislav, who hadn't seen her in ages. Lord knew how grumpy Bronislav would be if he missed a visit from his sister.

Dad agreed. They'd stay in Slovakia for three more weeks, as planned.

The phone call to Gabe was much shorter and contained a vastly different message, something along the lines of *if you show up, I'll kick your ass.*

Victor handed the phone to Ivan.

"Is there anyone else you should call?" Ivan asked, not bothering to pocket his phone. "You've been out of it for a few days. If there's a girlfriend in the picture, she might want to know you're okay."

"If I did have a woman, she wouldn't have a cell phone."

"Or teeth."

Vic grunted.

It wasn't an outright laugh, but Ivan was willing to take what he could get. He glanced down at his phone to check the time. It was long past dinner. "Are you hungry?"

"Not for hospital food."

"They brought ham casserole for dinner. It wasn't bad." The meal wasn't good, either, but Ivan had eaten everything, even the stale roll, to delay his headache. "I got you something better to sink your teeth into."

He wheeled a portable tray table to the bed, opened the small fridge in the corner of the room, and gave Victor a bona fide Italian hoagie from Hungry Hank's. "This is the best sandwich in town. Eat."

A spark of interest lit Victor's ravaged face. He lifted one half of the sandwich, opened his mouth, and winced. He touched the tight clump of stitches near the corner of his mouth and lowered the sandwich.

Gutted that his gift of food had inadvertently caused pain, Ivan stepped out of the room and found some eating utensils near the nurses' station. He returned and handed Vic a fork and knife. "Might as well eat like a civilized man. First time for everything, right?"

The joke fell flat on the cold, tile floor.

Victor cut the hoagie into small bites and began to eat.

Ivan opened up his laptop to check his email. There were ten messages from the computer engineering loop. Three notes from Stanwick, Bones, and Smitty wondering where he was. And one urgent plea from someone who wanted to buy one of his patents. He answered all of them, grateful for the diversion.

"What about you?"

"Hm?" Damn, Vic had only eaten a third of his meal. Under normal circumstances, he'd wolf down two large hoagies for dinner. Maybe three.

Vic peered at Ivan through one bleary eye. "You got a girl?"

Misery rose in his throat like hot bile. "No."

"What about that neighbor of yours? Your ears turned bright red when you saw her. That only happens when you're rattled."

"She definitely rattles me, but I graduate in a few weeks. There's no sense in starting something this late in the game." Especially after Tia received that text. A text that she believed right away. She thought he was a raging alcoholic who terrorized his ex, but only one part of that was right.

Now Tia knew he had a temper. A bad one. He'd lashed out at her like some self-righteous bastard. He felt like shit for how he'd behaved. That wasn't all, though. Tia knew about the restraining order. She'd heard the rumors about him. So had her colleagues. His past was back again, front and center. He could no longer pretend he hadn't done something incredibly stupid.

Someone at The Women's Grid was still spreading rumors about him, which meant he had to shut them down. He'd missed his appointment with the Dean in order to be at the hospital, but he'd reschedule that meeting. In a few days, he'd ask the administration to defund any non-inclusive program. The University would feel a lot of pressure to consider the request, particularly if he showed them the thousands of signatures on Stanwick's petition.

Problem was, his personal vendetta would affect Tia's program, too. If he didn't protect her, he'd prove he didn't have a heart.

Static burst from a speaker in the hallway. "Visiting hours end in fifteen minutes."

Ivan rolled the tray out of the way and noticed the knife was missing, but decided not to ask Vic for the utensil. Ever since his brother joined the military, he always had a knife on him. If a dull hospital dinner knife made him feel normal, then fine.

Ready to spend another night dozing in Vic's hospital room, Ivan settled back into The Heinous Chair. The nurses would let him stay. He was strong enough to hold

Victor down when the nightmares happened. Painkillers did that to Vic. They also made him puke. Not a good combination.

Victor peered at him. "Go home."

"I'd rather stick around and watch the Bruins game."

"You look like shit. Get some sleep."

"Don't need sleep." He just needed his brother to be well again.

"You've been with me for, what, three straight days? Four? Get out of here."

"Nope."

Vic pointed a long finger at the door. "*Go.*"

"Not a chance."

"For the love of fuck," Victor growled, curling both hands into fists. "Hemorrhoids go away faster than you do."

"Your ass is mine, bro. I'm not leaving."

"Yes, you are. Go home, take a shower, and get a decent meal. Don't worry about me. I'm not gonna take any more painkillers. Those little bastards make me feel worse than a one day weekend. I can sleep without them, but I can't rest with you beside me looking like death on a popsicle stick." Victor's voice lowered to a gruff murmur. "So go. Get some rest, little bear."

"Aw, hell. You haven't called me that in years." And even though so much time had passed, Vic was still taking care of him, still sending him to bed to get some decent sleep. Ivan wrapped an arm around his brother's shoulders and felt fourteen years old again, holding tight to all that solid bulk while everything fell apart. "I love you."

Victor gripped the back of Ivan's neck. "You're a fucking pain in the ass."

In other words, *I love you, too.*

Grief bolted into Ivan, carried on the thin wire of truth that had been slowly choking him for months.

No one knew who he really was, not even Victor. Ivan hadn't told a soul what had really happened eight months ago. Hiding that truth was slowly turning him into the worst version of himself. One who'd walk away from the only woman who ever wanted to read him right.

Chapter Fifteen

Tia's tea tasted like the pale liquid that seeps from a soggy pretzel, but she took another sip and watched another group of students enter the Campus Café. After a few minutes, she spotted Pamela near the coffee bar. The pretty blonde placed an order and headed toward a small table in the corner of the room. The dark circles under her eyes were gone. A rosy flush tinted her cheeks.

A good-looking guy settled into the chair beside Pamela and said something that made her smile. That man had to be Greg, her boyfriend. No, make that her fiancé. He looked huge. A football player, to be sure. One who'd ditched steroids to become a better person. For Pamela.

Approaching her in the crowded café wasn't a great option, but Pamela hadn't requested another counseling session and Tia was running out of time. The semester would end soon, and then Pamela would leave. It was now or never.

Tia walked across the room and stopped at their table. "Hi."

Pamela looked up. Her smile dissolved into ashen shock.

Her fiancé noticed the abrupt change and put his arm along the back of her chair the way guys do when they're worried about someone. He regarded Tia, but no recognition sparked in his gaze.

Evidently, Greg didn't know she was Pamela's counselor. This wasn't unusual. A lot of students kept quiet about their visits to the Counseling Center.

Tia chose her words carefully in order to protect Pamela's privacy. "I'm sorry for interrupting. I just wanted to thank you, Pamela. I've spent a lot of time thinking about what you said to me a little while ago. I'm grateful you were so honest."

"You are?" Pamela hunched her shoulders in a brief wince. "You're not mad at me?"

"Not at all. I'm glad we spoke that day." Because Tia finally realized that she needed to trust her instincts. She'd sensed that Pamela was telling the truth about the dark circles under her eyes, yet pushed for answers because she wasn't sure. For her, trusting the way she read people was the trickiest part about being a psychologist. "I'll remember what you said to me. I want to make sure I'm a good friend to the people I know."

"Oh. Good." Pamela exhaled. She smoothed out the paper napkin she'd wadded in her hand and gestured to her left. "This is Greg, by the way."

"It's nice to meet you. I'm Tia." She extended a hand, surprised by Greg's warm handshake and friendly smile. This was an awkward way to meet, but she liked the guy.

"Greg decided to study law here at Albrecht University," Pamela said with a shy grin. "That way, he'll be on campus while I finish my senior year. We're going to get married after I graduate."

"Congratulations. I wish you both every happiness." Tia meant every word. She wanted these two to have a happily ever after. "Well, I'll let you get back to your coffee. I'm glad I got to know you, Pamela."

"Me, too. And, um, thanks. For everything."

Relieved to step away on good terms, Tia headed outside into the warm air that had finally filtered into Vermont. Thin blades of green grass poked through the mud, thanks to seven straight days of sunshine. She'd been keeping track of every good thing in an effort to stay positive. Her spirits had risen considerably a few hours ago, when she'd gotten word that the post-doctoral position in Denver was hers.

She'd finish the final part of her training near the mountains she loved. Those snowy peaks were nothing like the flat Texas town where she grew up. Living near the Rocky Mountains for the next stage of her life felt like a good way to make sure her future wouldn't resemble her lonely past.

That loneliness had returned since she'd walked out of Ivan's apartment so many days ago.

He's a raging alcoholic. Stay away from that asshole.

Staying away from him was easy, because he wasn't

around.

Was he a raging alcoholic? She didn't think so. Yes, he definitely had a temper, but she'd never seen him reach for a drop of alcohol, not even to soothe his obvious worry for his brother. Instead of needing a drink to dull the pain, Ivan needed her.

Until now.

He hadn't reached out to her since Wayne's text. She'd tried calling but Ivan hadn't picked up. She had better luck with the two texts she'd sent. He responded both times, with answers that were short and to the point.

Vic has an infection.

Vic needs more surgery.

Clearly, Ivan had his hands full taking care of his brother. Was he taking care of himself?

A chill crystalized along Tia's spine, as icy as sleet. She scanned the graduate student parking lot, but didn't see Sturdy Stella. Looked like Ivan would be spending another evening at the hospital instead of at home.

She took the path toward their apartment building, aware of a couple heading the same way. The man was tall and forbidding. The woman was a stunning blonde who seemed completely at ease in his company. They both carried grocery bags packed with food.

Tia hurried forward. "Let me get the door for you."

"Thanks." The blonde smiled.

Tia stopped in the lobby to collect her mail. The man and woman started up the stairs the way couples did, side-by-side.

"It's been a long day," the man said. "I wanna get you

back to the hotel."

"Okay, but isn't it a little early for sleep?"

The stern set of the man's mouth eased into a lopsided grin. "Who said anything about sleep, Milenka?"

A happy laughed bubbled out of the woman. "I love you."

"Right. Good."

Whatever he said next was too low for Tia to hear, which was probably a good thing. The obvious love between them made her grin and ache at the same time. She tucked her mail into her bag and tossed an unwanted flier in the recycling bin, half listening to the couple's conversation as they headed upstairs.

"Why was he so angry at you?"

"Because I didn't listen when he told me not to show up at the hospital."

Tia yanked her gaze up to the man. His sturdy build resembled Ivan's broad frame, but his skin was a dark, nutty color. The woman looked golden brown, too.

Wait, that made sense. Ivan had said that his brother had taken his wife to Hawaii. They must've come back to check on Victor.

Tia started climbing the stairs. By the time she got to the second floor, the couple had already reached Ivan's apartment.

"...figure out what he needs," the man was saying as he opened the door. "Hell, he needs a lot. This place is empty."

The woman peered inside. "Where's he going to sleep if he gives the bedroom to Victor?"

"On the floor, probably." The man blew out a breath and pulled a hand through his hair. "We should get him a futon."

"Manchester Furniture has a good selection," Tia offered.

Both of them turned to look at her. The man raised one eyebrow, like Ivan sometimes did.

"You'll find their store on Maple Street. They've got good prices and fast delivery. That's where most graduate students shop for furniture." Oh, great. She sounded like an infomercial spokesperson. A nervous one. "I'm Tia, by the way. Ivan's neighbor."

"I'm Leigh." The blonde lowered her bag to the floor and gave the man's arm a fond caress. "My husband, Gabe, is Ivan's brother. We decided to drop off some groceries while Ivan is proctoring an exam."

"I'd better get this food into the fridge." Gabe hoisted the food into his arms and nodded a goodbye on his way into the apartment.

Leigh remained in the hallway. "You said that store was on Maple Street, right? Manchester something."

"Yes. Manchester Furniture." Tia closed her fingers around reassuring weight of her keys. "I've noticed that Ivan hasn't been around. I imagine he's been spending a lot of time at the hospital. How is Victor?"

"He needed another surgery on his eye, but he'll be discharged tomorrow. He'll stay here until he's strong enough to go home. We're going to make a bunch of meals so Ivan and Vic will have something to eat for the next few days." Leigh picked up her bag and smiled.

"Thanks for your help."

"You're welcome. I hope Victor feels better, soon." Tia opened her door and walked inside. Quiet surrounded her, carried in air scented by cinnamon.

Home. Her refuge. The place where she could escape all of the painful confessions she'd heard over the past eight hours. Listening to those painful confessions was the burden—and privilege—of being a psychologist. Every day, distressed individuals came to her and burst into tears. They'd reveal the terrible things people did to one another. They'd confide all of the fears and worries they couldn't share with anyone else. Every agonizing secret scraped a layer off her heart. There were times when she longed to see some love in this world.

She saw it, now.

That love was right next door, among the Antonovs.

They came running when one of them needed help. They came home early from vacations, brought much-needed groceries, and purchased furniture without being asked. They gave up high school football and forfeited the chance to pursue an athletic scholarship so they could take care of a frightened little brother. They wouldn't leave the ones they loved, no matter what. They'd stay long past hospital visiting hours, insist on sleeping on the floor so a sick brother could have a bed, and wouldn't let go until someone felt better.

All of this steadfast devotion came from men. Antonov men. And the one who lived next door hadn't gotten anywhere near her since she'd offered to listen to his side of the story about the restraining order. Tia longed to know why.

Perhaps Ivan was just like her.

He kept secrets, too. And those secrets were quietly tearing him apart.

CHAPTER SIXTEEN

Over the next few days, Tia poured all of her energy into work. She needed to find one more individual to sit on the Entrepreneurs in Technology panel. The first person that came to mind was Rebecca Danforth, the founder of Phoros Technologies. She was the woman Ivan wanted to work for. Tia called Rebecca to see if she'd like to be a part of the seminar, and received an enthusiastic yes.

As she got to know the inspirational stories of every woman on the panel, Tia began to have a change of heart about how she'd designed the seminar. She wanted to give everyone a chance to be a part of the discussion, so she managed to book one of the larger auditoriums in the Student Center at the last minute, opened the registration to whoever wanted to attend, and finalized last minute details.

Somehow, though, opening the seminar to everyone didn't feel like enough. Men were signing up to attend, which was wonderful, but they'd interact with the panel. They wouldn't interact with her, aside from the times she'd facilitate the discussion.

If she really wanted to be a psychologist who could help everyone, she needed to counsel men too. But how? Not many guys sought help at the Counseling Center. Those who did usually asked to see Wayne. There wouldn't be many opportunities to work with new patients after final exams, because most students would leave campus.

She could invite men to attend the SelfWell female sexuality seminar. Overall, the program wasn't about sex. It was about encouraging people to take care of their own needs. That could go for women and men. And if the discussion veered off into The Female Climax And How To Get It, she could share a list of resources that might help.

The thought of inviting men into such an intimate discussion made Tia's heart pound in her throat. A swallow didn't ease the flutter of fear that she might misread someone, but she needed to take this risk if she wanted to grow. It was time to step out of her comfort zone.

Excited by the challenge and nervous as heck, she entered her apartment building, took the stairs to the second floor, and stopped.

A body sprawled in the hallway, facedown and motionless.

Tia hurried forward and knelt beside a large shoulder. "Are you okay?"

The man grunted. Burly arms pushed a substantial

torso off the floor. A thick leg bent, planting one knee on the hall's floor. He pushed himself onto hands and knees and stopped as though the effort to get on all fours had drained what little energy he had left. Wet patches of sweat bled through his dark T-shirt. Brown dirt smudged the thigh of his black jeans. Black hair hung like a heavy curtain across most of his face. He looked like one huge bruise.

Tia recognized the long legs and long hair. "Victor?"

He nodded. At least, that's what she thought he did. It was hard to tell. The brief jerk of his head could've been a yes or a no.

"Do you need any help?" Of course, he did. His arms shook with the effort to hold himself up, but that didn't stop him from rising in one swift, awkward push off the floor.

She rose, too, and stared straight into the center of a chest that contained enough room for three hearts. This guy was huge. And chalky gray. And swaying. "You'd better sit down before you fall down."

He lurched toward Ivan's apartment.

Tia followed, feeling like a twig next to a massive sequoia. There was no way she'd stop him if he went down. If she got too close, she might get squashed under the thick trunk of his body.

Somehow, he managed to shove a key into the lock. As soon as the door swung open, he stumbled into Ivan's apartment and lowered himself into the dinged-up folding chair beside the old card table. He thudded two elbows on the table, speared ten fingers into his hair, and went as quiet as a body in a coffin.

Something was definitely wrong. If this man was anything like his brother, he'd probably gone too long without food.

Tia rushed into the kitchen. There was nothing inside the fridge except for a gallon of milk and a few condiments. Milk would have to do. As she poured some into a glass, she noticed a couple of prescription bottles on the counter. A precise, handwritten chart kept track of when each medicine had to be taken. Victor's next painkiller should've been taken thirty minutes ago.

No wonder he looked miserable.

She carried the cold glass of milk to him. "Here. A drink might help. This was all I could find."

A hand that was the size of a rotisserie chicken grabbed the glass. Dark scabs crisscrossed wide knuckles. A sick, bluish-green bruise bloomed near his wrist. The car accident had definitely done a number on this man.

"Do you need some medicine?" Tia gestured toward the counter. "According to that chart, you're due for a painkiller."

"I'm not taking that shit anymore." He held the cold glass against his forehead. "Oxycodone makes me puke."

"Oh. Maybe that's a good thing. There's less of a danger getting addicted to opioids if you can't stomach the stuff. Can you take something else, like an ibuprofen?"

"No." He moved the glass of milk to another spot on his forehead and murmured, "Thanks, though."

She nodded, not sure if he was looking at her. All she could see was wavy black hair, a nose that was bigger than most, and a hint of white gauze.

After a long moment, he chugged the milk and set the glass on the table.

Now what? Tia looked around. There was a gray futon couch in the living room, as well as a floor lamp. A neatly folded green comforter hung over the back of the futon and a pillow rested on the cushion. Tortoiseshell glasses perched on the stark storage trunk that served as a coffee table. Or nightstand, in this case. The living room had become Ivan's bedroom, and she was standing in it, soaking in every detail, looking for some clue that might reveal why he wouldn't talk to her.

A gurgling howl rose, the same type of noise Ivan's stomach made whenever he needed a meal. Tia looked at Victor, who yanked his gaze away from her and bent his head until all of that hair covered his face like an iron shield.

Years had passed since she'd felt hungry and alone, but she remembered that desolate feeling deep in her bones. If this man needed something to eat, he wouldn't find anything in the kitchen. Whatever food that had been in the fridge was gone. There was nothing left except for a half-empty bottle of yellow mustard.

Yuck.

"Hang tight. I'll be right back." She trotted to her apartment, fetched the leftover enchiladas she'd saved from last night, and returned to find Victor right where she'd left him, alone at the wobbly table.

One dark eye peered at her through a thick hank of hair. The fierce slant of his cheekbones, firm ridge of his brow, and wild tangle of long hair made him look ferocious, but the quiet way he gazed at her seemed almost shy. Or maybe careful, as if he didn't want to do anything that might startle her.

Finding him in the hallway had startled her more than anything else, but he seemed a little better now. Not as pale.

"Dinner will be ready in a minute." She put two big enchiladas on a plate and heated the food in a microwave that appeared to get more use than the stove. Didn't take long to find Ivan's meager collection of silverware. She grabbed a fork when the microwave dinged and placed the warm meal in front of Victor.

That's when she got a good look at his face. His cheekbones were fierce slants, his brow a firm ridge mirrored by a square jaw. A bright, red line ran from the corner of his mouth, up his cheek, and under the white patch that protected his injured eye. The cut reappeared above the eye, splitting his left eyebrow in two. The wound had to be at least eight inches long, held together by precise stitches. Those black threads looked ominous against the long, puckered gash. Eventually, with the right treatment, the shocking laceration would become a thin scar.

"Get a good eyeful?" Victor growled.

"Yes. Doctor Yung must've been on duty the night of your accident. She does great work. I saw what she can do when I volunteered at the hospital a few months ago." Tia propped her hands on her hips and nodded. "You look good."

His forehead bunched, twisting the ruddy cut that split his eyebrow. "I look like a demented pirate."

"No, not demented. You look fierce. Might be because you're hungry enough to eat a pirate's ship." Tia poked Victor's big shoulder. "Dig in, Captain Hook."

Victor narrowed his good eye and picked up the fork.

"I'll get more milk." She headed for the kitchen and heard the metallic scrape of a key slide into a lock.

Oh, no.

Not now.

Her heart kicked between her ribs like a mouse stuck halfway through a small hole. Tia froze near the fridge, but that did no good. There was no place to go. Nowhere to hide.

The apartment door swung wide open. Ivan stepped inside and frowned. "Something smells good."

"We've got company." Victor pointed the fork toward Tia.

Blue eyes swooped toward her. The sturdy length of Ivan's body went rigid.

Heat spurted into her face. A gloomy echo of the *you, me, us* thing bounced into her brain. *You, sucker-punched by surprise. Me, embarrassed and confused. Us, no longer together.*

Awkward silence billowed, as stale as cigarette smoke.

"I found your brother sprawled face-down in the hallway," Tia explained. "I followed him inside and fed him."

Victor glared at her.

She glared back. "That's what happened, right?"

The edge of his mouth turned up as though she'd said something funny. With a lazy shrug, he resumed eating.

"Did he pass out?" Ivan asked between clenched teeth.

"No, but he was pale and woozy. I think he needed food." Like most Antonovs, it seemed.

Ivan pulled a hand down his face. "Where'd you go, Vic?"

"Into town. On foot. I would've driven if you'd left the car keys." Victor scooped another forkful of food into his mouth and chewed slowly, like a docile bull in the middle of a sunny field.

"I told you to stay put," Ivan grouched. "Why didn't you wait until I got home?"

"I needed to call someone." Victor cut another piece of enchilada. "Took a while to find a phone. Not many payphones around here."

"That's because everyone has cell phones." Ivan tossed his onto the table. "Take mine."

Victor shoved the phone away from his plate. "I don't want your cell."

"You're getting it, and you're taking it every time you step out of my apartment. If you're going to go rogue on me, carry something that'll give you a way to call my lab if you need a ride or if you're about to pass out." Ivan shoved the phone back toward his brother. "Use this the next time you have to call someone."

"Don't need it. I already found a phone and called Bailey."

"Why Bailey, of all people?"

"Because he needs help." Victor shoved another forkful

of enchilada into his mouth. "He wants to hire you."

Ivan glowered at his brother. "I've already got a job."

"No, you don't. You took a shit job in Scranton instead of the one you wanted. Work for Bailey. In Boston."

"Not interested. I'm moving to Scranton. That's where I want to be."

"Bullshit. You're taking that job in Scranton so you can keep an eye on me." Victor curled one meaty hand into a fist that shook. "I don't need you, dammit."

"Too bad, because I need you. That's why I'm taking the job. I need to be close to family, okay? No big deal."

Whenever Ivan said *no big deal*, it was a big deal. Tia could tell this was a huge deal. He'd tossed aside his dream job so he could keep an eye on Victor, but there was no sign of regret or despair along Ivan's mighty frame. His shoulders were two rocks on his granite spine, all solid determination to stand by the brother he loved.

And here she was, watching them lob gruff accusations at each another like this was some tennis match. On silent feet, she moved past both men to the door.

"Tia, wait." Ivan looked at her, his expression grim. "There's something you should know. I've been working with the people who signed that petition against campus programs like yours. A formal request for a policy change might happen in a few days."

Tia's stomach clenched. "What kind of policy change?"

"A fair one."

"Fair to who?"

"Good question." He took a deep breath and rubbed the back of his neck.

Would this group of people pressure the university to shut down every program that wasn't inclusive? How would they define inclusive? Did they plan to target specific events that were closed to men, or would they attack any department that hosted these events? Was the Counseling Center in trouble?

Probably. Why else would Ivan tell her this? Did some of these people think her women-only seminars were as bad as the hateful ones offered by The Women's Grid? Did Ivan think so? All of these questions tumbled around in her brain, but she needed to know one thing more than anything else. "Are you okay?"

His gaze jerked to her. "What?"

"I haven't seen you in a while. How are you doing?" Now that she was finally able to look at him, she saw bloodshot eyes that contained a hollow pain. The two wide slashes of his cheekbones were pronounced against skin that had lost some of its ruddiness. Within the rich browns and golds of his whiskers, his mouth looked dry and chapped. Mountain Man was almost as exhausted as his brother.

Victor stopped chewing and peered at Ivan. "You look dead on your feet."

"I'm fine."

Tia didn't think so. Ivan was a walking advertisement for How To Be Wiped Out And Still Look Hot. Very hot. Hot enough to remind her all of the wonderful, lurid things he'd done to her in his bed. And the hottest thing of all was his unwavering dedication to the things he cared about: his brother, his work, and the causes he believed in. No question, that dedication came at a cost. He'd been going nonstop for the past ten days on very little sleep.

If she didn't do something, there was a very good chance she'd find Ivan passed out in the hallway the next time she came home. That alarming possibility drove a hard punch into her chest. "You must have a lot to handle right now. I can make dinner for both of you if that would help."

"God, no. You don't have to do that." Ivan braced a hand on the back of Victor's chair and frowned at the barren kitchen. "Dinner isn't a problem. I've got this."

Yes, he'd take care of everything. His brother. His work. His colleagues. Ivan was a man who didn't walk away from the people who needed him. He'd look after everyone and ignore his own needs, because that's what he did. She could read him, now.

She was so sure of what she saw, she decided to trust him...even if Wayne and The Women's Grid and his ex didn't.

"My invitation is still open," she said, worried by the bleak fatigue on both men's faces. "Dinner is on me all week, for both of you. If you're hungry, stop by at six o'clock."

CHAPTER SEVENTEEN

Four days later, bright blue signs appeared everywhere on campus, tacked to bulletin boards, taped to lampposts, and slapped on every door. Tia stopped to read the one posted on the Counseling Center's entrance.

Over five thousand people have signed a petition.

That's a lot of voices with something important to say.

Hear their message today at one o'clock in the Engineering Quad.

Would this be the announcement that Ivan mentioned a few days ago? Most likely. Tia walked toward the quad, aware of many others heading in the same direction. The quadrangle was packed with students, all facing the steps that led up to Harris Hall. A podium was set up in front of the building's wide doors. Two large audio speakers pointed toward the quadrangle.

Tia stopped near the edge of the crowd. A loud hum of conversation filled the air, punctuated by a few laughs.

A taut sense of expectation strummed through her veins.

The wide doors to Harris Hall opened, and Ivan appeared. Gone were the faded jeans he normally wore. A navy blue suit jacket hugged the broad width of his shoulders and a white button-down shirt was open at the collar, revealing the swarthy column of his throat. His beard was short and neatly trimmed, as always. The coarse silk of those whiskers was a heartbreaking reminder of the coarse hair that grew all over him. On his chest. Along his arms. Down the strong curve of his thighs. She'd touched all of those spots on the night she'd slept in his bed. Had that been ten days ago? Felt like ten years.

He'd gotten a haircut, and the short style made him look like a spokesperson, not a Mountain Man. Seeing him this way felt like he'd given away a piece of himself to the group who'd signed the petition.

Always giving, this man.

He strode to the podium and spoke into the microphone. "Over the past few months, a number of groups on campus have offered seminars that were open to women, but not men. Some of these seminars featured speakers who alleged that men are cruel, violent creatures who seek to dominate women in all facts of life: in the classroom, at work, and in relationships. Many of us were outraged by these assertions. We wanted to silence these voices, dismantle these groups, and end these outrageous attacks. However, that's not the right thing to do. The right thing to do is to preserve the freedom to say, and think, what we believe. We must allow these groups and these discussions to continue."

This was a surprise. Weeks ago, Ivan wanted to stop The Grid's hateful agenda. For some reason, though, he'd changed his mind. Anxious to read him right, she studied the straight line of his shoulders, the grip of his hand along the edge of the podium, the steady earnestness of his gaze. Whatever he was about to say was vitally important to him.

"Over five thousand of us have signed a petition against groups that don't allow men to participate," Ivan continued. "Our goal is simple. We want the freedom to examine and discuss every topic that is presented on campus. If you want Albrecht University to be a place where you have the freedom to discuss an issue, join us. Encourage the administration to ask every program that is funded by the university to open their events to all students. Give everyone a chance to hear, understand, and discuss the issues that affect our community. Thank you."

Wayne Hoover moved into the spot beside her and huffed. "That jerk is such a hypocrite. He started this whole men versus women thing on campus."

"You're wrong. Groups like The Women's Grid stirred up this unrest when they launched an all-out war against men. Ivan could've pressured the administration to defund The Grid, but he didn't. Rather than silence voices or ban groups, he preserved our freedom of speech. He was fair, firm, and inspiring."

"Inspiring?" Wayne rolled his eyes. "Don't you see what's going to happen? The administration is going to butt its big nose into every program it funds. They won't care that some of us have designed programs to address the unique needs of various populations on campus. Some bureaucrat will tell us to offer our seminars to everyone."

"I've already taken that step, Wayne. I presented the Entrepreneurs in Technology seminar to men and women on Tuesday. There were a couple of hiccups, but it went well. In a few days, I'm running a co-ed seminar on female sexuality in order to reach out to whoever might need help."

"Why? Don't you want to help women? Isn't that what drives you?"

"Yes, but I'm not going to shut men out."

"If you want to muddle your goals, go ahead. I'm targeting the people I want to help." He crossed his arms over his chest as his mouth tilted into a sneer. "That's all I care about."

"All you care about is yourself." She dodged a red-faced, belligerent Wayne and got up on her toes to search for Ivan. There he was, near the bottom of the steps. She hurried toward him. The crowd closed around her. Her hair snagged on someone's backpack. A twinge pinged at a small spot of her scalp, right above her ear, and then the peg of pain was gone. So were a few strands of her hair.

A kaleidoscope of movement turned around her, winter-pale faces lit by the warm blaze of April sunshine. Her foot landed on something flat and flimsy. She looked down and spotted a small poster someone had discarded. Mud splattered across words scrawled in black magic marker: *Let Dicks In.*

Whoever brought the poster had moved on to another crusade, which didn't seem right. A quest shouldn't be tossed aside and forgotten. Ivan hadn't forgotten his quest, even in the chaotic aftermath of his brother's accident. In the end, though, his solution was a complete surprise. He'd found a way to let everyone win.

She had to speak to him, now. It was unlikely he'd show up to her apartment for dinner. He hadn't done so for the past four nights. This might be her only chance to thank him.

Darting past a knot of people, she got caught in a stream of students who walked away from the quad. Tia tried to lunge out of the throng, but bumped into a group of sorority sisters who nudged her further down the sidewalk. By the time she stumbled out of the pack, she couldn't find Ivan.

Tia craned her neck, spotting him near a tree. "Ivan, wait!"

He paused and turned his head. The instant his gaze landed on her, he halted.

So did she, stunned by the deep smudge of exhaustion beneath his eyes. The stern slab of his forehead had two tense lines above his dark eyebrows, a clear indication that speaking to the crowd of restless students hadn't been something he relished. There was no hint of the dimples she'd once seen within the precisely trimmed whiskers of his beard. Every magnificent inch of his broad shoulders stretched the dark fabric of his suit jacket, his shirt bright white and so unlike the faded denim he usually wore. He looked stalwart and honorable, the kind of man everyone would admire.

He'd look that way even if he was dressed in a T-shirt and shorts.

"I want to thank you for the things you said a few minutes ago," she said. "It couldn't have been easy to stand up for free speech, particularly when a group like The Women's Grid is likely to bring in more speakers who might say awful things, but I think you did the right thing."

"The Grid isn't the only group capable of doing awful things. I know guys who are just as bad. They're the ones who put those outrageous signs in the residential quad a few weeks ago. Once I thought about that, I began to search for a different solution to the problem."

"I see."

He stiffened. "What, exactly, do you see?"

"I see *you*, Ivan. You stick with the causes you believe in. You stay with the people who need you. You do the right thing, even if that means you have to give away a piece of yourself." She nodded, trusting her instincts about this man. "You have a heart that's twice as big as Texas. Believe me, that's a huge heart."

Someone bumped into her, jabbing a sharp elbow into her lower back. The push knocked her off balance.

Ivan grabbed her arm and glared at whoever stood behind her. "Watch it."

"Sorry. My bad." Elbow Guy stepped closer, a notepad clasped in his hand. "Can I ask you a few questions for an article for the campus newspaper?"

"Not now."

"I just need two minutes of your time." The guy's mouth drooped like a sad Bassett hound. "I don't want to talk to anyone else. You're the only one who makes sense about the petition."

A skinny man with a dark moustache nudged the Elbow Guy aside. "Ivan, we need to go back to the lab."

"Hold on, Mr. Antonov." A woman dressed in a severe gray suit stepped forward. "The President of the University wants to talk to you, right away."

Tia watched Ivan's expression flatten. He was trapped by too many obligations that couldn't wait. He had scads of people to help, graduate work to finish, a brother to look out for, and a new job to think about, which meant he had to find a place to live after graduation. This man had too much to do.

She walked away, determined not to be something else Ivan had to take care of. Fortunately, she could take care of herself. That's what self-sufficient people did. After all, she was one of the lucky ones. She'd learned how to trust her instincts.

One of these days, she'd learn how to deal with the heartache of being without the only man who'd encouraged her to believe in those instincts.

CHAPTER EIGHTEEN

Ivan rubbed the back of his head. Didn't do any good. Nothing could remove the dagger of tension lodged in the base of his skull. Not food. Not sleep. Not even work.

Taking care of a belligerent brother who was as big as a battle tank was no easy thing. Ivan had spent most of the past five days worrying about Victor. Grading tests. Trying to convince Victor to rest. Wrapping up research. Freaking out when Victor refused to answer the phone. Dealing with students who didn't have a clue. Listening to Victor threaten to leave. Searching online for a place to live in Scranton. Keeping a sharp eye on Victor's wound to make sure the laceration didn't show signs of infection. Proctoring all of the evening exams while Stanwick, Bones, and Smitty scrambled to finish their final projects.

At least he didn't have to worry about feeding his brother. Thanks to Tia's generous offer to cook dinner, Victor just had to go next door for a decent meal. No, make that a stellar meal.

Knowing Victor, he probably ended up in the kitchen with Tia, standing side-by-side and boiling onions or whatever the hell cooks did. Vic wouldn't say much, but Tia would draw him out in that gentle way of hers. If he started to talk about anything, he'd end up being funny and likeable. Wouldn't take long for Tia to realize Victor was two hundred and ninety pounds of perfect.

Shit.

Ivan lumbered into the lab and dropped into a chair.

Henry stopped typing. "Whoa. Looks like you're having a sucktacular day."

"I just spent the past hour and a half with the President, the Provost, and the Dean of Students. That guy never shuts up. He wouldn't let me leave until I agreed to show up at some pointless committee meeting next week."

"Lucky you."

"Yeah, that's me. Lucky." Ivan opened his laptop and scrolled through the text messages he'd routed to his computer. A couple of students wanted to know if they could get an extension on their final projects. Someone wanted to know how many people were going to show up at the engineering department's year-end picnic next weekend. And an urgent message from Stanwick that said *Yo, Antonov. Can you figure out how I can finish building my robotics project with my arm in a cast?*

The dagger in Ivan's head turned into an axe.

Smitty plowed into the room, his wooly black mustache all aquiver. "Where have you been? Have you forgotten about grading the projects from the Comp 101 class?"

"I graded everything submitted by the students in my section." He'd gone through those assignments last night, hunched over a computer in the lab rather than going home to sleep on his cozy new futon.

"You finished grading all of that? I'm impressed." A hopeful smile sprung beneath Smitty's stache. "Listen, can you look at some of the projects in my section? I'm swamped and could use some help. You're fast enough to grade quite a few projects in an hour or two."

Doubtful. He barely had the energy to slump in his chair. Ivan squinted at the digital clock on his screen until the blurry numbers came into focus. Five forty-nine.

Bones sauntered in and plunked a scrawny hip on the edge of Ivan's desk. "There's another bug in the Aurora software. None of us can figure out what's going on. Professor McNeil wants you to take a look."

Ivan braced his elbows on either side of his laptop, lowered his head, and dug his hands into his hair. He'd worked hard to be needed like this. Lately, though, every time someone came to him, they only seemed to want his brain.

Except Tia.

She came to him every time he needed her. Even after she'd learned the worst about him, she came up to him to say thanks for how he'd handled the petition. That wasn't all. She'd looked past the rumors and lies, deep enough to see his heart.

He shoved his laptop into his knapsack. "I'm going home."

Smitty blinked. "But you just got here."

"I've been here for the past two years." Ivan stood.

Bones scowled. "What about the bug in the Aurora software?"

"You'll find it." Debugging the program wouldn't be easy, but Bones would manage if he sat still for more than fifteen minutes.

Stanwick burst into the room, cradling his broken arm as if he'd just returned from the emergency room. "Oh, thank God. You're back."

"*No.*" Ivan shouldered past him.

"Don't you want to know what's wrong?"

"I already know what's wrong. I've worked fifteen-hour days for the past eight months. I want a life."

"Hallelujah and amen, brother. It's about fucking time." Henry stood and clapped. His one-man standing ovation echoed off the room's concrete walls and rendered Smitty, Bones, and Stanwick speechless.

Ivan gave Henry a brief salute and strode out of the lab. By the time he burst out of Harris Hall, he'd stuffed the only suit jacket he owned into his backpack and loosened the collar of his button-down shirt. He walked fast, pounding the soles of his scuffed shoes against the sidewalk.

A window on the second floor of Decator Hall screeched open and someone yelled, "Circuit Theory SUUUUUUUUUCKS!"

An electrical engineering textbook sailed out of the window and landed in a bush. A sparrow flew out, startling a few students who sat on the grass, studying for final exams under the lowering sun. A guy dressed in a Sigma Chi T-shirt spotted him and waved. "Hey, do you have a second?"

No, he didn't. Ivan kept walking and glanced at the clock on the library's tower. Five minutes to six.

Frat boy caught up. So did the smell of stale beer on his breath. "I overslept and missed the review session this morning. Can you explain a priority queue algorithm to me?"

"Ask someone else." Ivan broke into a jog, the seam of his slacks rough against his inner thighs. He darted onto the gravel shortcut that led to graduate housing but knew he was too late. Ten days had passed since he'd walked out on Tia.

All because of his stupid pride, because he didn't want to admit he wasn't as smart as he was supposed to be. Fuck smart. He wanted her, wanted to feel her slim length against him, wanted her brightness to light up his dark nights, wanted to be with the only woman who knew him better than anyone else.

The six-story brick apartment building loomed ahead, a stark peak of hope in the flat landscape of his life. Her car was in the usual spot, the dent no longer visible on the door as if he'd never touched her SUV.

As if he'd never touched her.

He trotted into the building, sprinted up the stairs, and pounded on her door. It swung open to reveal Victor.

His shoulders were as straight as ever and he wore his usual uniform of black jeans paired with a black T-shirt. The only thing different was his hair, which hung in a long black curtain across the left side of his face. Before the accident, Vic always pulled his hair into a man-bun. Not anymore.

At least his eye was okay. They'd gone to see the ophthalmologist a few days ago to remove the bandage, and the scratch on Vic's cornea had healed. Victor could see out of both eyes, now. Which probably explained why he'd spent so much time at Tia's place. She was the best thing to look at on planet Earth.

Ivan cleared his throat and tried to sound casual. "I'm here for dinner."

Victor nodded and sauntered over to the couch as if he owned the place. He pointed a remote at the TV to turn down the volume on some cooking show.

Ivan crossed the threshold and got a mouthwatering whiff of butter and garlic. He looked toward the empty kitchen. "Where's Tia?"

"At Annette's."

So, Vic was on a first-name basis with her friends. Fine. No big deal.

Ivan lowered his backpack to the floor and looked around. Tia's place had changed. A potted plant sat where his teacup used to be on the coffee table. Two bright patterned pillows rested on the couch. One pillow was smushed, presumably from Victor's big bulk. The dining table was set for two, with white plates on blue placemats. A small bouquet of flowers filled a glass bowl. Looked like a romantic dinner was about to happen.

A hard roll of nausea tumbled into his stomach.

Tia stepped into the apartment with her nose buried in a cookbook. "I found a flan recipe. Do you think I can get away with heavy cream instead of condensed milk?"

"No. Stick with condensed milk." Victor waved a hand toward Ivan. "Looks like we'll need another plate."

"Hm?" Tia looked up. "Oh. Hi."

Her hair was pulled back in some sort of braid that highlighted every inch of her pretty face. A hint of pink gloss tinted her mouth. She was in jeans and a rosy blouse, the first splash of color he'd ever seen her wear. Maybe being with Victor brought that out of her.

Now that she was within reach, he couldn't speak. The muscles along his forearms twitched with the need to pull her close. The swollen knuckle on his right hand throbbed with every hard thud of his pulse. All of his thoughts scrambled into pixels, indecipherable and indistinct.

"Now that everyone is here, I should take the salmon out of the oven." Tia hurried into the kitchen.

Victor ambled to a cabinet and returned with another plate and placemat, setting them on the table like any good host would do for an unexpected guest.

Ivan gestured toward the flowers. "What are these for?"

His brother shrugged and sat at the table. "Cop a squat. You're blocking my view of the TV."

"Screw that. Did you bring these flowers?"

"Hell, no. I brought a recipe for salmon. Now sit down. I want to watch Bobby Flay make chipotle mayonnaise." Victor pointed to the lanky man on the television screen. "Chef Flay is a god. Tia met him, once."

Sounded like Tia and Victor had bonded over food, the one topic Ivan knew nothing about. Great. Wonderful.

She emerged from the kitchen with a plate of salmon in one hand and a big bowl in the other. When she placed the food on the table, she looked at Ivan. "Would you like water, iced tea, or milk?"

Her. He wanted her, but a hot burst of emotion closed off his throat. He hadn't been able to talk, really talk, ever since the night she got that fucking text.

"He likes milk with dinner," Victor said, serving the salmon.

Tia nodded. "Be right back."

Ivan lowered himself into a chair and peered into the steamy bowl. "Good lord. She made risotto."

"You should've come last night. She made fettuccine alfredo. The night before was macaroni and cheese. Night before that, lasagna." Victor placed a buttery slab of salmon on Ivan's plate. "I think she's trying to fatten us up."

She'd also made food that was soft and easily chewed so that Victor's stitched-up mouth could finally eat. Her thoughtful menu had worked. Victor looked like he'd put on a few of the pounds he'd lost. The color had returned to his olive skin. And the mangled corner of Victor's mouth contained a curve of contentment.

Ivan swallowed, hard. How would he ever thank Tia for this?

She walked out of the kitchen, placed a glass of milk near Ivan's plate, and sat across from him.

The heady scent of her home cooked meal was nothing compared to the power of her presence. Now that he was three feet away from her, his frozen insides rebooted. His heart pounded in hard, powerful jolts. His fingers twitched with the memory of her silky skin, his body ached for her touch, his mind reeled with the memory of how she'd clung to him when she'd climaxed. She'd given him all of those precious things even though he'd had nothing but one thin pillow to share with her.

Didn't seem right. All his life, he had to give to get anything.

Until Tia.

"Final exams began yesterday." She pointed warm brown eyes at him. "Will you have a lot of tests to grade?"

"Yeah." Three hundred and twenty-four, to be exact. And that was just for the Computer 101 class. He'd split them up with the rest of the department's teaching assistants, but he'd do the lion's share of the grading if necessary. Everyone around here depended on his intellect, and he was willing to share his gift because being smart was easy. Being himself wasn't. Whenever he opened up, he couldn't control the ferocity of his emotions.

Like the wretched moment he'd bellowed at Tia for asking about the restraining order. After she'd read that awful text about him, she had every right to wonder if she'd made a horrible mistake. Hell, she'd just gotten out of his bed when she realized he might be a monster. He'd never forget her wide-eyed shock when she'd looked at him or the way her hands shook as she held her phone close to her chest. In spite of her obvious distress, she'd offered to hear his side of the story.

If he told her everything, he'd have to admit that he'd failed in every possible way.

Victor dumped a spoonful of sugar into his iced tea and nudged the small bowl of sugar to Tia, who sprinkled some into her drink. The small interaction spoke volumes. After just a few days, his brother knew how to meet Tia's needs.

Jealousy wrapped an oily hand around Ivan's neck. Hating that choking feeling, he shoveled a forkful of salmon into his mouth.

"I rented a car," Victor said.

Ivan stopped chewing. "Why do you need a car?"

"It's time to go home." Victor took a drink of iced tea as though he hadn't dropped an armed grenade in the middle of dinner.

A wad of salmon stuck in Ivan's throat. He forced the food down with a hasty gulp of milk. "No, Vic. You need more time to heal."

"I can't spend any more time lying around. Trout season is in full swing, which means people are returning to the lake. I've got to get back to my restaurant." Victor ate the last bit of his risotto and glanced at Tia. "Like I told you, yesterday."

Since when did Victor spill his guts to anyone? Ivan dropped his fork. The silverware hit the plate with a loud clank that mimicked the clang of alarm in his chest.

Tia swallowed her mouthful of food. "I know you want to get back to work, but I hoped you'd stay a little longer. Didn't one of your waitresses find someone to run the kitchen so you could recuperate?"

"I need to make sure he's a decent chef. If he sucks, he'll drive away customers. I can't let that happen. I've worked my ass off to build a good reputation. If this new guy doesn't produce quality food, my restaurant will be in serious trouble."

"I understand. But take things slowly, okay?"

"Got it." He reached halfway to Tia's arm, stopped, and balled his hand near her placemat. "Thanks for everything."

"You're welcome." She put her hand on Victor's big fist, brushed the long drape of hair away from his face with a gentle caress, and kissed his scarred cheek.

The emotionless mask fell from Victor's demolished face. Shock widened his eyes, followed by a heavy beat of want.

Ivan stood, heartsick and ready to tackle his brother if necessary. "You can't drive home while you're on pain medication."

"I stopped taking those meds days ago." Victor rose, looming over the table like a skyscraper.

Ivan grabbed him by the wrist. "I've been watching those pills disappear from the prescription bottle on the counter. You've been taking them, one every six hours."

"Wrong. I've been throwing them away every six hours because you pitch a fit when I don't take them."

"Are you kidding me? Damn it, Vic, I don't want you to be in pain." But Ivan could see that Victor had buried his agony once again. One of these days, that massive chest wouldn't be able to contain any more hurt. "Give yourself one more week to recover."

"I know you've got my six, but I don't need backup." Victor pulled free from Ivan's firm hold. "I left your phone on the counter."

"Wait, damn it." Ivan grabbed the thick curve of his brother's arm and pulled him in close until their chests bumped.

Victor's back went as stiff as a knife hilt.

Yeah, his brother was definitely off painkillers. If he was still taking those blasted pills, Vic might've hugged back. Ivan gave him a hard squeeze and let go. "See you soon."

That didn't even get a grunt of acknowledgement.

Ivan's eyes prickled. Damned contacts. "Call when you get home, all right? And buy a cell phone."

Victor walked out and closed the door behind him with a firm pull. Whenever he closed a door like that, he wasn't coming back.

Didn't matter. In a short while, Ivan would follow. No closed door would stop him. He'd make sure Victor healed, inside and out. Like Vic had done for him.

Ivan walked into the living room to stare out the sliding glass door. All of the snow had melted from the parking lot. The grass along the sidewalk was starting to turn green. Spring had finally reached Vermont. He hadn't even noticed until now.

Tia came to stand beside him.

"It hurts to see him go," Ivan admitted, watching Victor walk across the parking lot. "He can leave the ones he loves. Always has. He takes off on purpose, I think."

"Maybe he's walking away because he doesn't want to burden you with his problems."

"Too bad. He's not getting rid of me." Ivan paid close attention as his brother slowly eased into a nondescript sedan and drove out of sight.

Tia began to clear the table. The clink of dishes sounded like goodbye. Dinner was over. Time to leave.

He didn't want to return to his empty life. He didn't want to be just a brain and nothing else. He wanted Tia, and the only way to earn a shot with her was to do something meaningful, something he'd hadn't done before. He had to tell her everything.

"Her name was Stacy," he said, turning toward Tia. "We met in college. She's the one who filed a restraining order against me."

Tia stopped stacking dishes. "You don't have to tell me this."

"You deserve the truth."

"I know the truth." She wiped her hands on a napkin, as calm as could be. "I know you."

"No, you don't. You need to know what happened."

"That's not what I need." She tossed the napkin to the table.

His mouth went dirt dry and his palms went wet as mud. "Are you talking about Vic? Is he the one you need? I don't know how close you two got over the past week, but I can tell he wants you. He's never talked to anyone like he talks to you."

She shook her head. "Your brother is a wonderful man, but he left."

"Just say the word and he'll be back."

"You're probably right. You're right about most things, except for this." She tapped her chest. "I don't need to hear any explanations. You've already told me what happened. Your ex filed a restraining order against you. A judge dismissed it. You didn't do anything wrong."

"But I did. Stacy and I had a hellacious fight. I asked her to move out. She refused. I felt so friggin' trapped, I couldn't take it anymore. I sucked down a six-pack of beer and threw a bottle against the wall. A shard of glass cut her. She didn't need stitches, but she bled. I did that to her."

"Yes, you did." Tia's eyes hardened into two dark stones. "You never meant to hit her. I know this. I know you. You don't have to tell me more."

"Really? Now you don't want to hear my side of the story? What the fuck, Tia?"

"You're not telling me your side of the story. All you're doing is going through the timeline of what happened, which is fine. I can listen to that if you want, but I'd rather hear the real stuff." She propped both hands on her hips. "What's eating at you, Ivan? What keeps you up at night? What do you think about when you can't sleep?"

"Rumors. All of them. They echo in my brain. Around here, everyone believes I'm an alcoholic with an anger problem. They're wrong. I'm not an alcoholic. I don't drink, except for that one night. What I really am is the type of man who leaves someone when she's at her lowest, when she needs me the most."

"But she wasn't giving you what you needed," Tia insisted. "What did you need?"

"Freedom. I couldn't take her depression any longer. She complained all the time. And the mood swings. God, the smallest things would set her off. One day, she noticed a small kink in the carpet and had a total meltdown. Nothing made her happy except for planning her wedding, but I didn't want to be her groom. I just wanted to leave."

"That freedom cost you, didn't it?"

"Hell, yes." God, this woman. She read him so well.

"How much did it cost you?"

"Everything. Hell, I would've chewed off my own foot to get free, but I handled things quietly. She was already depressed. I didn't want to make things worse for her. The only friends she had were the ones she knew at The Women's Grid, and none of them could stand me. They thought I was a heartless bastard for asking Stacy to move out of my apartment. They still do."

Tia plucked the serving spoon out of the risotto and pointed the round end at him. "You protected Stacy, even when she allowed her friends to stomp on your good name. How does that make you feel?"

"Angry."

"You can do better than that, Mountain Man." She poked the spoon into his chest. "Tell me how you really feel."

"Pissed off. Mad as hell. Just thinking about it makes me insane. I can't escape those rumors, those lies. They're always there, eating at me." *This.* He needed this. He needed to get the venom out. He yanked the gooey spoon out of her hand. "I wanna throw this fucking thing at the fucking wall."

"Don't." Tia grabbed him by the shirt, crushing the fabric in her fists. "Tell me why. Why are you so mad?"

"Because I gave her everything. I paid her bills and took care of her and practically laid down and died for her and when I couldn't take it anymore, she took everything I had, even my frigging toothbrush, and there was nothing I could do to fight back because she was sick. I had to take it like a pussy because she wasn't herself. And you know what? She dragged me through the dirt and stomped on my good name and lied about me to her friends, who've talked smack about me ever since. *That's* what I got for trying to do the right thing, and it's not fucking fair."

"Exactly. I couldn't have said it better." She released him and stepped back.

"Oh, no you don't." He waved the spoon at her. "I'm not done yet."

"Not at all. There's a ton of rage buried inside you. If you can get it out, you might finally be able to get some decent sleep."

"I don't care about sleep." He tossed the spoon aside, but he was shaking so hard the throw went sideways. The spoon careened off a chair and flicked risotto onto his slacks. "You believed the rumors, too." His voice cracked. His throat hurt. Everything hurt. "One text, that's all it took, and you looked at me like you didn't really know who I was."

"I know. I did that." She pressed her lips into a firm line. "That text surprised me."

More emotions rose, hard and hot inside his ribs. "You believed the lies. You believed them instead of me."

"No, I believed *you*." She pointed to him. "*You* confirmed that someone filed a restraining order, remember?"

"Yeah, I confirmed it all right. I yelled. No, I screamed at you, and you flinched. You looked so pale, so…" Wide-eyed and trembling. Stunned and hurt. *Shit*. He pushed the heel of his hand against the tight spot of pressure in his chest. "I scared you. That destroyed me. When I walked away, I thought you'd never come near me again. But you did. You called. You sent texts to ask how I was doing.

You helped my brother. You offered to help me. You even thanked me. You came to me when I was too gutted to reach out for help. That's what you did. That's what you always do. You give me priceless things like that, all the time. God, Tia. I love you. I love everything about you."

She covered her mouth with her hand. The light winked off her ring like a spark.

That spark lit him up, made him say everything. "All my life, people wanted me because I was smart. My friends knew I was the guy who could fix their computers or find a string of busted code. My professors knew I could do a ton of research for them. My girlfriends knew I could figure out what they wanted. You don't need any of those things from me, but I'll give them to you anyway. I'll give you everything I have."

"No, Ivan." Her eyes filled with tears. "You don't have to give me everything."

"Too late. All of me is yours." He stepped close enough to see the gold flecks in her dark brown eyes. This woman was a treasure he'd never expected to unearth in the personal hell of his regrets. "You're the only one who can see my heart. It's yours."

"That's all I want." She yanked him into a hug and kissed him.

Soft, satin lips. Those loving hands in his hair. Full breasts pressed against his racing heart. Every stellar inch of her nestled against him. Joy burst inside him, bright and glittering. He locked his arms around her and dove into the kiss, all that heat and light, and finally he was free, no longer trapped in a dark cave of anger. He could tell this woman how he really felt and she'd hold him close, kiss him like his heart was the best thing about him, not his brain.

"I want you more than I ever wanted that job at Phoros," he growled, sliding a hand down to cup her ass and pull her tight against him. "I need you more than I need food."

"*Ivan.* You're the one I want. Only you." She kissed him again, tugging at his shirt as if she couldn't get close enough.

The hot sugar of her mouth was the best thing he'd ever tasted, because he could feel the echo of her words on those sweet lips. She wanted him, no one else but him. She saw him, really saw him, and now she was in his arms, holding tight, giving him the one thing he always wanted. He grabbed the thick rope of her braid and kissed his way down to the triangle of freckles below her throat. Beneath his lips, he felt her chest rise and fall with fast breaths. At this angle, with her blouse dipping low, he caught a glimpse of her breasts, round flesh cupped by pink satin.

Wait, pink?

"Your bra matches your shirt." He ran a finger along the open neckline of her blouse, staring at her curves. "I've never seen you wear pink."

"It's because of you. When you lost that volleyball game, I won a decent chunk of change and spent that money on lingerie. I haven't been able to buy new bras in ages." She blushed and unbuttoned her blouse with a shy flick of her fingers. "I've been dying to show you."

"The next time you want to show me new lingerie, don't wait. Call me and let me know where you are. I swear to

God, I'll answer. I'll drop everything and come to you. I'll meet you at the mall, I'll sprint into the store, and I'll sneak into the dressing room on my hands and knees for the chance to see you wearing next to nothing."

She laughed and stroked her fingertips along his beard. "I love the way you talk when you're happy."

"Honey, I'm jubilant." He wanted her so badly, he shook with sharp, hot need. It felt so good, this wanting, because he knew this woman wasn't going to take a piece of him. She was going to fuse him back together.

She loosened another button and backed away. "I want you, inside me. Hot and long and hard, pushing into that narrow spot you found when your hand was between my legs."

Everything inside him went hard, aggressive. "Yes. That."

"I don't have condoms, but I'm on birth control pills to regulate my period. I won't get pregnant."

Bareback. With Tia. "I'm clean, honey. I've always used condoms. If you want me to get one, there's some in my apartment."

"No. I want you. Just you." She unbuttoned her jeans. "In my bed?"

"Anywhere. I'm ready. Been ready for months. The first time I saw you in the parking lot, I was ready." He clawed at his shirt, the fabric stiff and annoying against his overheated skin.

"I've been thinking about you sprawled under my covers, dark against my white sheets." She unzipped her jeans and pushed the denim down.

He stared at the way that pink bra held up her breasts and wanted to grab her, squeeze her, do dirty, wonderful things to her. Then he spotted her tiny pink bikini panties and he growled, toggling into full caveman mode. "Come here, you."

"Nope. I want you under my covers, Mountain Man." She crooked a finger, turned, and walked toward her bedroom.

Her tawny ass cheeks were tight, round. A juicy peach wrapped in pink satin. He ripped off his shirt and prowled after her.

Inside her room, an electric candle glowed, throwing gold light over a bed covered in a thick, blue quilt. Tia smiled in welcome.

He grabbed her and cupped her breast, the satin bra cool against his hot hand. Her nipple was a hard tack beneath the fabric, begging to be touched. He rubbed her there and she arched toward him like she needed this, like she needed him. Hands shaking, he unhooked the clasp between her breasts and curled his hand around her luscious flesh, soft and round and sexy, God, so sexy, the way she rubbed against him, the little whimper in the back of her throat while he got reacquainted with those nipples, tickled those beautiful little peaks with his fingertips, pinched them a tiny little bit between his fingers.

Yeah, she was soft, but she was also long and lean, with a flat abdomen and graceful thighs that were cut with muscle. This woman was strong enough to handle him when he went caveman, when he needed to yell, or when he needed to bury himself deep inside.

He needed that. Right now. He yanked down his zipper and shoved his slacks down. The pants bunched around his ankles, an annoying tangle. He stepped on the fabric, stepped out of the clothes, kicked the rest out of the way and slammed his foot into her nightstand. The lamp wobbled. He stopped it from falling with a quick grab.

Tia grinned. "Good catch, babe."

He practically tossed her onto the bed and fell on top of her, groaning because she felt so good, silky smooth and loving, smiling lips and hungry hands, stroking his arms, his back, his ass. Her panties were still on, which wasn't right. He tugged at them, trying not to rip them. "Off."

She didn't seem to mind his inability to form complete sentences. After a little wiggle, she removed the panties and pulled him close. The tip of his dick touched slick heat. His nipples went hot and hard, drilling into her soft flesh. Hot lust flooded him. He anchored his weight on his forearms, spread her legs wider with his thigh, and pressed his hips forward until his cock sank into tight, wet heat. It was so good, the edge of his vision went dim.

"My love," she murmured against his mouth.

Hers. He was all hers. He pushed deeper, taking her body inch by mind-bending inch, the fit getting snugger. Sweat rose across his back with the effort to go slow, be gentle. He kissed her, a soft silent promise that he'd do whatever it took to keep this, *this*, this sacred thing that he needed more than the next beat of his heart, and kissed a path down to her sweet tits, licking until her nipples became a bright red while his dick ached inside all of that slick wet skin.

He worked his way back up to her mouth and felt her wet, hot nipples against his chest. Felt good. He pushed forward, wanting more wet, more hot, more tight.

She gasped. "Yes, there."

He felt it, too, that delicious clench in the spot where she got narrow and sensitive. That tight place that had driven her wild when he'd rubbed it with his fingers. His cock was eager to do the same. Stroke by stroke, the rhythm of Ivan's hips echoed his pounding heart. His body, his mind, everything was hers. He angled his hips to drive deeper, to lock himself to her.

"*Ivan.*" She shuddered and closed her eyes.

He initiated another kiss but it quickly fell apart, her mouth opening in soft, fast pants as she met his thrusts. A pink flush bloomed along her cheeks. She was turning the same beautiful pink as her nipples, her sex, all of those secret feminine parts he'd discovered, and suddenly he understood that he was the one who'd put the color back in her. The bright blouse and rosy bra and the pink blush were all his.

To finally have her was too much. His body switched from give to take. Pleasure stroked him all the way from the corners of his mouth to the back of his calves. Every thrust drove him deeper, tighter, until there was no turning back. His lab could explode into flames, the mainframe could chew up his entire thesis, the campus could sink into a fiery pit and none of those things would pull him away from Tia.

Because everything he did meant nothing without her. Her hips bucked, her fingers dug into his back, and an orgasm squeezed her body around him, turning his glittering pleasure into something incandescent. His climax detonated, so intense he became a liquid thing, pouring into her until he had nothing left. Satisfaction rolled over him like water and he was drowning, happy to die like this. In her arms, buried deep inside her body.

Understood.

Needed for all the right reasons.

He panted against her hair as the aftereffects of their lovemaking still clenched her sex around his in soft, diminishing pulses that sent shivers into his balls. Hell, he should say something, tell her how much she meant to him, but he had no words.

A throaty, satisfied sigh came out of her. She beamed up at him. "I don't think I've ever seen you speechless."

He laughed. "Give me a minute."

"Take your time." She stroked his neck, his jaw, his beard. "Even after you make love to me, I can't keep my hands off you."

"Keep your hands on me. Always." He turned his head to give her better access to his neck and caught a glimpse of something blue on her nightstand. His teacup. The little duck bobbed inside, peering over the edge. "We're being watched."

"Hm? Oh, the duck. I had to move him in here a few days ago. Victor almost broke the teacup the first night he showed up for dinner. I think he was nervous."

Ivan looked down at her, unable to withhold the truth. "He was nervous because he wanted to be with you. Victor thinks you're better than butter."

A small smile inched across her kiss-softened lips. "He might've liked being fussed over and fed."

"That's not all he liked."

"I liked him, too, but I've got a thing for a hot computer guy who takes me to weird movies and makes love like a Mountain Man." She looped one leg around his hip, her thigh like satin against his ass.

He grinned, happy to be trapped between her lovely legs. "I plan to take you to weird movies and make love to you for the next thousand years."

Some of the carefree light faded from Tia's eyes. "There's something you should know. I've been thinking about what to do after my internship ends in July, and it's a little complicated. I got the post-doc position in Denver."

Shit. They'd be sixteen hundred miles apart, but he could drive up to the airport in Wilkes-Barre and fly directly to Denver. "I know the distance between us won't be ideal, but I'll come out to see you."

"But I—"

He cut her off with a kiss. "Every weekend. Holidays, too."

She went still beneath him. "Ivan, no. That'll cost too much money."

What, exactly, was she saying? He frowned down at her. "I'll be able to afford it."

"No, Ivan. I refuse to be a burden to you. Flights to Denver aren't cheap. Some are five hundred dollars, round trip." She shook her head. "That's too much money."

His stomach dropped, a hard slap against his gut. "I don't give a rip how much—"

"Stop, Ivan. This is non-negotiable. Nothing will change my mind. I want to have a happy life. And my life is a thousand times happier when I'm with you, which is why I'm going to find a job in Scranton." The fierce determination in her gaze melted into something warm and bright. She bestowed a kiss on his lips that tasted like a promise. "It'll be you and me, together."

Ivan exhaled into a happy smile. "Us."

CHAPTER NINETEEN

Being part of an 'us' had never worked for Tia. When her father left, she and her mom became an 'us' who struggled to pay the bills. When they paired up with another single mother and her daughters, that version of 'us' had more financial stability but less peace and quiet. The next 'us' was with her college boyfriend, who was fond of her but eventually flunked out because he rarely studied. Other versions of 'us' with other men never lasted.

Until Ivan.

With him, promises were always kept. He moved to Scranton to watch over his wounded brother, just as he said he would. He'd tell Tia he'd call after dinner, and he did, eager to hear about her day. He'd offer to make the four-hour drive to Vermont to visit, and he'd arrive in three and a half hours because he couldn't wait to see her.

Weekends with Ivan contained toe-curling sex and a

surprising amount of laughter. This man loved to make her laugh. He loved to be outdoors, which wasn't a big surprise, and introduced her to his favorite pastime, which involved fishing on any lake he could find. But he also wanted to be a part of her world, so he willingly attended yoga class and never minded being the only guy in a roomful of her girlfriends. He could finish a five-hundred page book in one day and seemed to know how everything worked, but he always made her feel smart. And needed. And oh, so loved.

For these reasons and more, Tia moved to Pennsylvania in August. She found a cute apartment in Scranton and a good post-doctoral job at a well-respected psychology practice. By the end of the summer, she was doing meaningful work and beginning to adjust to Life With The Antonovs. Victor usually ended up at Ivan's house on Friday nights, and tonight was no different. His rusty white pickup was already parked in the driveway.

Tia parked next to Ivan's new SUV and checked her appearance in the rearview mirror. Her eyeliner had smeared during the long drive home. She rubbed away the smudge, applied a fresh dab of lip gloss, and walked into Ivan's house without knocking. After a brief search, she found him in the kitchen.

He stood by the stove, dressed in the chocolate brown slacks he'd worn to work. A tan oxford shirt clung to the impressive width of his back and his thick hair had almost grown long enough to reach the back of his collar. The sheer size of him seemed to take up most of the kitchen, six foot two inches of powerful male with a huge heart.

Her heart sped up at the sight of him. Her Mountain Man had learned to cook over the past few months so she wouldn't have to shoulder that chore alone, and he'd already mastered a few dishes. He'd produced some disasters too, but those flops were adorable. Tia hadn't thought spaghetti could catch fire, but Ivan had managed to find a way. Tonight, the smoke alarm was silent, so whatever he was cooking would probably be a winner.

She drew close and inhaled the mouthwatering scents of chicken, butter, and garlic. "Dinner smells great."

His face lit up with the smile he only had for her, the one that produced two divots in his beard. He put his arm around her waist, tugging her close for a soft kiss. "Damn, I missed you."

"Missed you, too. Good thing the conference in New York is only once a year. I hated being away." She stroked his back. The thick plate of muscle along his shoulder blades contained three hard knots, a sign that something was wrong. Tia looked up at him. "How are you?"

He shrugged and resumed ladling sauce over the chicken. "Will you be on call this weekend?"

"Nope. All I have to do is stop by my apartment for some clean clothes. Want to spend the weekend at the lake?"

That got a brusque nod and nothing else. Yep, something was definitely wrong. Tia longed to know what troubled him, but Ivan grew quiet when Victor stepped into the kitchen. The big guy didn't lift his head or meet her gaze, just stared at the floor as though he was waiting for the Travertine tile to crack beneath his big feet.

"Hi Victor," she said. "Want to join us for dinner?"

He shook his head. "Gotta work."

"But I thought you hired someone to cover the late shift."

"I fired him." He crossed his thick arms over his chest.

By now, she could read every Antonov. Each brother had a small tell that appeared whenever his emotions grew too intense. Gabe muttered 'right, good' whenever he felt unsettled. Ivan got too quiet. And Victor shook. He'd crossed his arms to hide the telltale shake in his hands, but Tia could read the tension that vibrated throughout his body. Even the ends of his hair quivered from the cool autumn breeze coming through the window.

She stepped toward him and peered into his face, or what little she could see through his long black hair. He hadn't shaved in months. Dark whiskers covered the lower half of his face as if he'd been stranded on a deserted island without a razor or a mirror. Even though he looked like a perilous pirate, he lived like a hermit. He spent all day in the hot kitchen of The Crab Trap and slept alone in the small apartment above his restaurant rather than face the wide-eyed stares people gave whenever they spotted his jagged red scar.

Whenever Tia looked at him, she saw his strength and selflessness.

His loneliness, too.

She got up on her toes and looped her arms around his shoulders in an affectionate hug, something she didn't do unless Ivan was close by.

Big arms wound around her waist, drawing her in

with gentle care. Victor bent his head to rest his grizzled cheek against hers, his breath warm against her skin. He stayed within her arms for a brief moment and then pulled away. Without another word, he left the kitchen. Two seconds later, the back door thudded shut.

Tia frowned. "Victor didn't say goodbye to you."

"He's not too happy with me right now."

"What's going on?"

"I'll tell you in a minute." He spooned some chicken and rice onto a plate.

Tia watched, fascinated by the swollen knuckle on his big hand. That hand could cup and stroke her so well. Her breasts perked up, begging for a little attention from that hand. Her nipples placed their request of attention, too, tingling for a soft pinch or maybe a warm suck from Ivan's handsome mouth. No, better leave that mouth alone so those lips could convey whatever was in his bottomless heart.

This man's capacity for love never ceased to amaze her.

She rested one hand on the taut curve of his butt, remembering the last time she'd clutched that cheek as his hips pumped into her. Heat pooled between her legs, igniting a pleasant swelling sensation deep inside her. Seven days without Ivan and she was ready to rip off his clothes in the kitchen and beg him to love her.

"Come with me, Boots." He picked up two full plates and walked past the counter where they normally ate.

She followed him in a horny fog. Those dark slacks clung to his backside like hot fudge on two scoops of ice cream. Took a minute to realize he'd led her into the dining room. The place wasn't empty, anymore. He'd gotten a table. Not just any table, though. It was the one she'd admired two weeks ago when they'd wandered through a furniture store. The long, rectangular top was stained a dark walnut, with thick pedestal legs that gave the piece a substantive, farmhouse feel. Ivan had bought the chairs, too. They were incredibly comfortable, with thick upholstery that enticed you to stay for a while and chat.

He set the plates down. "You liked this, so I bought it."

Just like he'd done with the roomy armchair she'd admired, the soft blue blanket she'd liked, and the massive four poster king-sized bed that had actually made her gasp in awe. He was filling his home with the things she loved.

Somehow, she had to stop him from doing that. Looked like she had to work harder to convince him to spend his money on stuff he liked, like fishing equipment or a new boat.

Ivan pulled out a chair for her. "We need to talk."

"Of course." She sat, wary of the firm jut of his jaw.

He sat beside her. "I got a promotion, Tia. They want me to produce a photovoltaic battery based on the research I did at Albrecht."

"That's wonderful." And not surprising at all. Ivan had a brilliant mind and a great way with people. This job opportunity would give him the chance to do the things he'd always wanted to do, so why didn't he look happy? "You're not smiling. I wish I knew why."

"Because this isn't working for me. You in your

apartment. Me in my house. That's not what I want." He looked up at her, his eyes so very blue.

Her dry tongue scraped against the back of her mouth. "What's wrong with us?"

"That's what I'm trying to figure out. A while ago, you mentioned that your father left your mother, but you never told me how that affected you. Things were difficult after he left, right? For a while, you probably had very little money. Without him, it must've been tough to pay rent, buy food. Women were the constant in your life, the ones who never failed you. You probably swore that you'd never do what your mother did and follow a man somewhere without making sure you could take care of yourself. That's why you got an apartment when you moved here." He raised an eyebrow.

"Yes, that's one reason why I got my own place. I didn't want to move in with you as soon as I got here because we haven't been together very long." They'd talked about where she'd live a couple of months ago. Why rehash this, now? She pressed her thumb against her ring, the smooth silver slippery against her damp skin.

Ivan took her hand. "You refuse to sleep over, yet you never complain when I stay at your place. Why?"

"My birth control pills are—"

"In your nightstand, which provides a convenient excuse for you to go home. You don't want to stay in my house."

He was right. There was a very good reason why she only stayed a couple of hours whenever she was here, but her good intentions had backfired. Ivan's eyes were pinched with pain, his shoulders a tight row of muscle and bone. This arrangement wasn't working for him, and that had to be fixed. *Now.*

With her heart pounding hard, she climbed into his lap. That produced a sharp frown along Ivan's broad forehead. He wasn't expecting her to get closer, which made her feel worse. The only thing she wanted was to be with this extraordinary man. She straddled him, not caring when her dress skidded high on her thighs. There wasn't time to dawdle. Any second now, he'd tell her that they needed to finish talking, but talking wouldn't work. She had to show him how she felt, so she unbuttoned his shirt and slid her hands inside to steal a touch of warm skin and crisp chest hair.

The breath came out of him in a hot huff. "Tia, I—"

She cut him off with a kiss and the tension in her belly dove low, coiling in a deep throb. His mouth was a slick, perfect thing. Wide lips framed by chocolate whiskers, so delicious she'd never get enough of his flavor. She slipped her tongue inside, a flirtatious flick along the roof of his mouth.

His hips jumped, bumping against her damp panties. The brusque thump of his body against hers was a welcome relief.

"More. I need more. Going seven days without you has left me hollow and desperate." She stroked the back of his strong neck and furrowed her fingers into his thick hair, clasping tight to hold him in place as her mouth reminded him that they were good together. That living separately could definitely work. She kissed him until they were both panting, and then nibbled along the precisely trimmed edge of his moustache, tiny little bites and tugs that made him groan and chase after her mouth with his.

Allowing him a deep kiss, she unbuttoned the rest of his shirt and raked her fingers down his torso until she found his belt buckle. A hard tug pulled the belt open. The fly of his slacks didn't stand a chance against her. Nothing would stop her from claiming the prize between his legs, and when she finally clasped the long, silky heat of him in her hand, she sighed. "You're spectacular."

"One touch from you and I'm harder than a hammer."

"Hot and strong. Like the rest of you. So good-looking, my thighs clench every time I look at you." She licked the hollow of his throat, one of the few places on his body that didn't have any hair and was baby soft. "I need your chest against mine, your hands on my ass, your cock deep inside me."

"Not yet. I'm not done talking." But his gaze went white-hot and he slid his hands under her dress to grab her ass.

"No, not here on the new furniture. I'll get everything wet." She scrambled off him and tugged his arm. "On the carpet. Dinner can wait."

He landed on the floor on one knee, his gaze sharp and lusty as she yanked off her clothes.

She nudged his shoulder. "On your back. Mm, yes. That's good. Half-undressed in your work clothes works for me."

"Works for me, too. My woman is going caveman on me." A smile broke across his mouth. "I think I'm having a moment."

"You'll be having more than a moment." She crawled on top of him and pinned his hands to the floor so she could rub all over him like she'd dreamed of doing all week in her lonely hotel room. His body was a hard slab of muscle, even bigger now that she'd had two months to make sure his belly was always full. The hair on his chest tickled her breasts, the whiskers on his face tickled her lips. His body was so very different from hers, coarse and hairy and brawny, but she'd found so many soft parts in this hard man.

The tender heart that beat for her.

The hollow of his throat that always had something good to say.

The velvet tip of his cock that filled her emptiness until she felt whole.

She canted her hips to welcome that part of him and slowly sank down, shivering when he hit that deep, narrow spot that sent a zing of sensation along her sex.

"I never understood men until I found you." She rose and sank again, wrapping her fingers around his wide wrists like handcuffs, wanting to claim him, take him forever. "I love you, Ivan. So very much."

He clenched his teeth. The veins stood out against his strong neck. "Let go, Tee. Let me touch you."

"Not yet." She threaded her fingers through his as pleasure grew taut within her. She bumped against him, faster and faster, as the tingles and trembles gathered, pulled, and climbed. Sex was always so good with Ivan. Fast or slow, up or down, in whatever position they ended up in, she could always feel his love pour into her.

The intensity of his gaze was as powerful as a stroke along her skin, and her orgasm came hard and deep, leaving her weak and breathless as Ivan groaned beneath her, caught up in his own climax.

She released his wrists and closed her eyes with a guilty wince. Even though she'd just taken him in a raw, selfish way, she wanted to do it all over again.

Ivan rolled over, pinning her beneath him. "You're scared. You're afraid this love of yours is going to back me into a dark corner, that I'm going to feel trapped, that I'll leave you like every other bastard has done."

Of course this man would figure her out. Nothing escaped his great mind. He was so tuned into her, he could spot her deepest fear. And now that she was beneath him, breathless and quivering, she had no way of hiding from the truth. She'd developed a dark, helpless need for him… just like his ex had done.

His ex had needed him so badly, he'd become desperate to get free. To regain his freedom, Ivan had been willing to lose everything. Tia couldn't do that to him. Ever. She dragged her hands off his bulging arms and dug her fingernails into the carpet. "I don't ever want to trap you in a dark spot you can't escape."

He shook his head, his eyes glimmering. "Every time you trap me, you free me. You prod me to go through some experiment I don't want any part of, and the heaviness inside me lifts. You handcuff me, and being close to you is the best thing I've ever done. You pin me to the floor and the pleasure you give makes me want to lock myself to you and throw away the key. Please, honey, move in with me. Light me up, every single day. Hang your clothes next to mine. Sleep beside me. Fill my cabinets with your teacups. Lie on the couch with me while I watch hockey. Let me teach you how to fish. Take me to your favorite yoga class. Decorate our house in shades of blue. Touch me whenever you want. Ask me to bring milk home when we're running low. Tell me you love me, because I need to hear that every day. Make love to me in my bed, in my shower, on my furniture. Buy a white dress and marry me soon, because being without you is fucking killing me."

A sharp arrow of emotion zinged deep into her sinuses. The pang expanded, making her entire face ache. Her vision blurred and hot tears rolled out of her eyes, not her nose.

Now that she was with Ivan, even crying was better.

"God, no. Boots, don't cry. Honey. *Shit*." He smoothed the hair away from her face and dropped kisses along the trail of her tears. "Vic was right. I should've waited to propose until you had more time to get used to the idea, but I couldn't wait. I didn't even ask for your hand. I demanded you marry me like some Neanderthal. Tee, honey, I'm sorry."

She slid her hands up the heavy contour of his chest, past the thick ridge of his collarbone where his skin was hot and warm. She cupped the back of his neck and looked at him, his blue eyes anguished and the shells of his ears a bright red. "Your proposal was perfect. Every time I see your raw emotions, I love what I see. Yes, I'll marry you."

He relaxed a little. "Soon, all right? Please. I don't want to wait. I can't. God, I love you."

"How soon?"

"Next week."

"Wow, Antonovs do marry in a hurry." She smiled, touched by his obvious desperation. "If you could give me two weeks, my mom will be able to get here for the ceremony. She'd like that. So would I."

"Anything that's important to you is important to me. We'll get married in two weeks." He kissed her, softly. "I'll find a preacher."

"I'll find a dress." As she lay on the wooly carpet with a cold dinner on the table and a warm man in her arms, she knew she'd finally found someone she could love, and need, forever. "Mind helping me move into your house, tonight?"

"Hell, yeah." His smile was wide enough to trigger the dimples on either side of his mouth. "First, we have to stop at the jewelry store. I need to buy a couple of rings for my wife. One will have a diamond as bright as she is, and the other one will have three words etched on the band." He lowered her mouth to her ear, his voice husky with emotion. "You. Me. Us."

"The End" feels so final. Please, let's keep in touch. You can join my quarterly newsletter or find me on your favorite social media platform. Say hi to me on Twitter, Facebook, Google +, Pinterest, Goodreads, and Instagram.

If you have a moment, please consider posting an honest review on the site where you purchased this book. I'd love to hear what you think about TURN TO HER.

About the Author

LYNN KELLAN believes men and women aren't that different—both want to be with someone who will empty the dishwasher. Lynn fills her contemporary romances with smart women who like to laugh and rugged men who will always offer to change a flat tire for a stranger. All of Lynn's heroes hide a secret, and they're searching for the woman who believes the sum of their strengths is greater than the depth of their flaws. Her books contain surprises, great sex, and the occasional bear who interrupts a passionate moment in a hot tub.

When Lynn isn't writing, she's playing golf with her husband, laughing with her two kids, and trying to get her Sheltie to stop barking. She has won multiple writing contests and served two full terms as President for her local Romance Writers of America chapter.

Subscribe to Lynn's newsletter for updates about new releases. (http://www.lynnkellan.com/contact.html)

For more information, visit:
LynnKellan.com

Also by Lynn Kellan

The Brothers Series
Run to Her — Book 1 — available now
Turn to Her — Book 2 — available now
Promised to Her — Book 3 — will be released in 2018

Anything You Ask
Convincing her to love him is the only way he can return home, but can she love a deaf man who was rejected by his own family? Awarded a 5-star TOP PICK review from The Romance Reviews and winner of the NJRW Golden Leaf Award for Best Novella

Clear as Glass
The last thing Mitchell Blake needs is another hotshot consultant to "save" his glassblowing factory, but this one is different. She is hiding something. If he can unearth Jaye's secrets, he might have good reason to fire her…or keep her forever. Winner of five Romance Writer of America chapter contests and finalist in the Book Buyers' Best contest.

Acknowledgements

Being a writer is a lonely business. In order to finish a book, months go by while you pound away at the computer. Sometimes, the only people you speak to are the characters inside your head and your dog. It's a sad day when you realize the dog doesn't give a hoot about goal, conflict, and motivation.

Fortunately, I'm blessed with the support of fellow authors who understand this weird compulsion to write. My critique group—Jackie Kelly, Renee Wynn, and Pat Leedom—I treasure you. Profound thanks also go to Alleigh Burrows, Chantel Clark, Adele Downs, Eileen Emerson, Veronica Forand, Kate Forest, Stephanie Julian, Piper Malone, and Susan Scott Shelley, who are always willing to provide feedback on the art and craft of writing romance. In addition, I'm grateful for every member of the Valley Forge Romance Writers. You are a constant source of friendship and inspiration to me.

Finally, I'd like to express thanks to my husband, who knows me better than anyone else and still sticks around. Now that this book is done, I owe you a cheesecake and a round of golf.